<u>Writer's Note:</u>

You may notice immediately that the order of the
chapters is a little mixed up, this is not an error,
I have written it this way on purpose.

Feel free to reread it again with the chapters numerically
if you wish.

Enjoy.

Acknowledgements

Everyone who continues to support me and my work.

DINNER PARTY

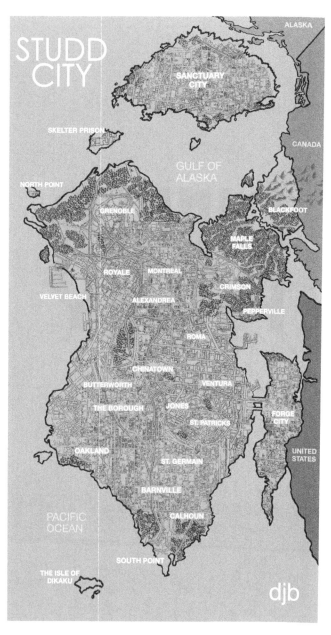

STUDD CITY

ALASKA

SANCTUARY CITY

SKELTER PRISON

CANADA

GULF OF ALASKA

NORTH POINT

GRENOBLE

BLACKFOOT

MAPLE FALLS

ROYALE   MONTREAL

CRIMSON

VELVET BEACH   ALEXANDREA

PEPPERVILLE

ROMA

CHINATOWN

BUTTERWORTH   VENTURA

THE BOROUGH   JONES

ST. PATRICKS

FORGE CITY

OAKLAND

ST. GERMAIN

UNITED STATES

BARNVILLE

PACIFIC OCEAN   CALHOUN

SOUTH POINT

THE ISLE OF DIKAKU

djb

It is a question that everyone has been asked at some time in their adult life.

"If you could invite any famous people, that are no longer with us to a Dinner Party, who would it be?"

So, who would you invite?

Chapter 11

Who the Fuck is Mary Magdalene

An abundance of stifled laughter can be heard from behind the confines of the bulky mahogany double doors. This evenings dinner party is in full flow and the sound of the guest's merriment bleeds through the yawning doors and spills out into the emptiness of the hallway.

The pleasant hubbub drifts and wanders around the high ceilings, brushing against the Gothic interior of the old house, like a lost spirit or spectre searching for a way out of limbo.

The variety of laughter and voices blend together, but seem to have a lack of feminine tones, just the slightest sound of a female's voice can be heard meandering gently, almost shyly through the coarse collection of male bombilation. Her soft inoffensive voice mingles in and out of the contrasting male voices, as though dancing together around the crystal chandelier that hangs from the high ceiling of the majestic hallway, as if the voice were being shared by numerous dance partners cutting in, almost courting her. As quickly as the sounds came, they evaporate at the top of the twisting staircase that leads into the darkness of the first floor and are replaced by yet more playful clamour. But even before the dance of the veiled voices can begin again, they are immediately overwhelmed by the vigorous marching of footsteps, as a waiter strides across the checkerboard tiled floor. His posture as straight and proud as a pencil, his beaklike nose pointing upwards, slicing through the air like the fin of a shark cuts through water. His arm held high and straight like the trunk of a tree, his slender fingers contorted like deformed branches as they balance a pewter tray on top, topped with a freshly retrieved and opened bottle of Syrah wine, the red interior appearing quite black in its dark glass confines. The waiter enters through the double doors releasing the unmuted conversations and saunters around the table to the man sitting at the head of the large oval shaped table, thoroughly enjoying the conversations that are taking place all around him. The waiter offers the bottle to him, displaying the wine's label, he replies with a nod and an arrogant flick of his hand, signalling to him that he may serve it to his waiting guests.

The mahogany wall panels and the fact that there are no windows gives the room a very uncomfortable sense of claustrophobia, and the various hand painted art pieces that hang on each panel do little to brighten such a dull interior. The only thing to battle the tedious decor is a gigantic poster of the 1956 movie 'Love me Tender' starring Elvis Presley. Elvis is seen holding an acoustic guitar as the centrepiece on a vanilla coloured background of the poster, the names Richard Egan,

Debra Paget and Elvis Presley emblazoned on it in a deep red, above Elvis' name are the words 'introducing' indicating this to be his debut film. With the dinner party in full swing, a gathering of flamboyant looking guests surround the table, that is draped in an elegant white cotton tablecloth, and places set for seven with the finest silver cutlery there is to offer. One place is set but is without a guest and with the napkin still expertly manipulated into the shape of a swan, it would appear that this particular guest was either running late or unable to attend the evening's festivities. But seemingly unfazed by this the other guests continue to enjoy the evening and continue to consume the starter, which happens to be chilled pea and chervil soup accompanied by Crème fraîche.

The illuminating glow of the chandelier glistens on the luxurious silverware, as it moves rapidly in unison with a clamouring shrill of cutlery on porcelain. The light is deflected from the dancing spoons and hurtles towards a tremendous gramophone that sits proudly on a solid cupboard that once again, match the theme of overwhelming mahogany. The gramophone flaunts its tremendous brass horn like a narcissistic peacock display. Married to it is a pile of old vinyl records, topped by the fifteenth studio album of Elvis Presley entitled 'From Elvis in Memphis'.

Each of the guests are at various stages of consumption, as too are the wine glasses containing red wine at various different levels. The waiter professionally makes his way around the table and fills up the glasses before leaving the room and closing the doors behind him.

The Host, who is a distinguished looking middle-aged gentleman with hair as black as soot but streaked by flashes of grey mirrored on both sides of his head. He smiles as he takes in the atmosphere, and enjoys the exuberant collection of guests as they are enthralled in conversation. He unknowingly strokes at his chiselled chin, a personal trait when he is deep in thought or concocting some scheme or game. His olive skin glistens without a single shard of facial hair, a shave so close it could only have been completed by a straight or cut-throat razor. He wears an immaculately pressed black tuxedo, a fresh red rose bulges from his button hole not yet ready to wilt as it quivers majestically like a flag topping a sandcastle. Suddenly he stops stroking his chin as if hit by a eureka moment and raising his glass to his lips. He sips his wine swilling it around his maw, savouring its dark fruity flavours with hints of blueberry and black olives seducing his taste buds. He swallows, and the flavour lingers before leaving behind the peppery aftertaste that one gets with Syrah. He lowers the glass back down, his tuxedo sleeve riding up to reveal an expensive looking gold-plated watch, slathered in what seems like hundreds of tiny twinkling diamonds. He glances around the table at his guests, who are at this moment in time lost in their own discussions and quite oblivious that their every word and mannerisms are being examined. To his left sits a man with an overwhelming resemblance to the legendary comedian, Groucho Marx.

At closer inspection it is clear that he is dressed and made up exactly the same as the late comedic great on purpose. Clad in a creased and crinkled black suit complete with a flower, void of almost all its petals, as if prior to the evenings first course he had been playing a game of 'she loves, she loves me not', but nonetheless it sits cultivated and displayed in a lapel planter. His hair is wavy and wild like jet black candy-floss, and of course the trademark pure Havana cigar drooping from his prised lips and getting doused in droplets of soup as he tries in vein to eat and keep his cigar in place. The round spectacles have also made an appearance but unfortunately fail to stay in place, sliding down a slender nose (not as bulbous as the real Groucho) but the treacle like grease paint is ever present in broad strokes over each eyebrow and over his lip like a sticky moustache. The Host surveys The Groucho, pauses at the nose situation and his left nostril flickers slightly as if in pretence that he will scowl, but thinks better of it knowing that nothing can be done about The Groucho's nose apart from emergency rhinoplasty and that is just ludicrous. He turns his attentions to the next guest around the table. On The Groucho's left hand side sits an Adolf Hitler look-alike. A sense of sympathy must caress one's mind for the bad hand that he has been dealt by God to look like such a despicable human being as Adolf Hitler. At closer inspection it appears that he is a lot younger than the true führer, a slender man in his mid-twenties, a short smart haircut, slicked back and tight to his skull, a layer of grease causing it to shine under the light of the hanging chandelier glow. The infamous toothbrush moustache, visibly a fake with the edges of the double sided adhesive protruding from either side. He is wearing a khaki coloured chancellor uniform, smartly pressed with flawless authenticity, topped with all the trimmings and finishing off the ensemble with a bright red armband wrapped snuggly around

12

his upper left arm, emblazoned with the symbol that brought fear and distress to thousands of innocent people, the swastika. On the table set off to the side of his soup bowl is his officer's cap, khaki to match his pristine uniform and peak in black, sheltered underneath are the fingertips of some brown leather gloves. Again, The Host's nose twitches, trembling for a couple of seconds, not completely satisfied with The Adolf's youthful appearance. He had pictured him older, but yet again there is nothing that can be done about this situation and concedes, knowing that he has the best doppelgänger's available. The next place homes an empty seat, the origami swan still sitting on top of the placemat waiting to be unravelled and placed on the missing guest's lap. His brow furrows with annoyance and suddenly he brings his fingers up to meet his temple, as if hit with a sudden migraine, wincing like he had been skewered with an ice-pick.

As the table curves, a lookalike to the late great Elvis Presley sits, eagerly tucking into his soup, lapping it off the spoon with all the finesse of a stray golden retriever. The thick green soup is flicked into air haphazardly and settles on various parts of his handsome defined jawline, the majority stopping at his dimpled chin. As he stops to talk, his bleached white teeth gleam, his unnatural tan giving them that extra pizzazz of light on dark. There is an illusion of a dark radiant glow to his bottled skin tone, but it fails to capture the tone of The King's Cherokee lineage. He smiles a cheeky smile in obvious flirtation with the female guest sitting to his left, pushing back several strands of hair that have fallen in front of his eye line. He runs his hand through his dyed black hair, which is combed back and obviously painstakingly caressed into a pompadour style standing high over his forehead, held in place by some heavy duty hair product. Completing the famous hairstyle are two sharp sideburns flashing down to his cheeks like twin flashes of lightning. His whole body is clad in black leather; a jacket zipped halfway down his torso exposes the muscular contours of his chest, the sleeves are pushed up tightly sitting just below the elbows, and two black leather bracelets are wrapped around his wrists. His look reminiscent of Elvis' outfit for his television performance in 1968 for his comeback special. The Host is pleased as punch with The Elvis, even a little aroused perhaps. A grin caressing his face like a salivating customer at a gentlemen's club having just seen his favourite stripper stride onto the stage and grasp the cold steel pole in her hand. The Host's hand excuses itself from the table and disappears into his crotch area. The Host was very pleased with The Elvis indeed. But the person The Elvis was flirting with? Well, a match made with these two would have been the stuff of dreams perhaps, it would be like the coming together of Zeus and Hera, Gods of our pop culture. The look-alike is of Marilyn Monroe. A beautiful woman with a natural glow, not overly made-up with make-up, but her plump lips are overwhelming in bright red like two plump moist raspberries. Her succulent lips frame two rows of perfect gleaming teeth, as she laughs loudly obviously enjoying the swaying conversation between herself and The Elvis. She picks at the wholemeal bread roll that compliments her soup, hollowing out its internal softness and placing it graciously into her mouth. The cloud-like texture of the bread, streaked with red like lashes from a whip as it brushes her lipstick. The trademark black mole protrudes from her left cheek; presumably fake, and the well-known platinum blonde hair flows as it should, styled in a windblown, soft waved fashion, too perfect to not be a hairpiece. To finish off the look, she wears the classic white halter dress, low-cut, revealing her curvaceous and alluring bosom. But tonight, there is no subway grate breeze present to recreate her iconic scene from 'Seven Year Itch'. The Host's eyes switch back and forth, from The Elvis and The Marilyn, almost watering at the mouth, quite clear that he would very much like to see a consummation between these two iconic stars of a past era. Maybe would like to be involved himself. Finally, on her left hand side, and The Host's right, sits a lookalike to Jesus Christ. The Host's face changes and the hand creeps back around the neck of his wine glass.

Is it a religious belief that brings his self-petting to a stop? A realisation of where he is? Or is it merely glancing at a religious figure such as Jesus (even though it is not really him) enough to halt masturbation mid stroke.

The Jesus is a young slim male; maybe around 25 years of age, looking way too young to portray the son of God if we're being honest. But with his long wavy, shoulder length brown hair and a full beard of the same colour, which conceals the lower part of his face, not at all groomed well or cultivated with a wildness to it as though it's been allowed to grow freely, like a clematis attaching itself to whatever it can and smothering it in every which way. He is shrouded in a long white linen robe, creased and uncared for, it is not known whether this was the look that

15

the person intended or just a lackadaisical approach to laundry. The Host's gaze hurries past The Jesus. With almost an embarrassed blush glowing in his cheeks. Could he really believe that this young man was Jesus Christ? Or could he? Had he really convinced himself that his guest was who they were pretending to be? Had he manipulated his mind that on this very evening he was playing host to the most outrageous and extravagant dinner party ever. Or is he himself playing a character in his own game? Becoming someone else and reacting to the situation how his character would? Time as they say, will tell.

"So what famous people would you all sleep with?" Comes the peculiar question from The Host, just pulling the trigger on one hell of an icebreaker.

The gathering looks on dumbfounded and wondering where he is going with this, wanting to look at each other, longing to make eye contact with the other guests to let them know that they're thinking the same thing, they're on the same page. This guy is nuts! But, it's his party, they're getting paid quadruple the amount that they normally get from these appearances, plus, the exquisite food. So, they give him the benefit of the doubt and they focus on him, he is obviously very passionate about the subject matter and the guests remain respectful and gently nod in agreement.

"I mean you have to take your time and think about a question like this." The Host continued "So, I thought about it and do you know I thought about it for almost three months!" He has them now, something about his calm and soothing voice, it's almost as if it lulls them into a state of trance. He has them right in the palm of his hand like a magician in the middle of some death defying illusion. They stare at The Host, they don't mean to, but they're all captivated by him, just something about his personality draws them in, hanging on his every word. The Host continues his tale sniggering and then laughing loudly shaking his head in his own disbelief of how this event came about.

"I must have gone through a small forest worth of paper, I just kept changing my mind!" he laughed.

"This is like a laminated list." The Elvis grins.

"Excuse me?" replies The Host wearing a mask of confusion.

"You know, a list of celebrities that you want to sleep with and your other half can't get mad." Says The Elvis smiling widely, his pearly whites stained pea green from the thick soup. The Host looks on a little annoyed at this unanticipated sidestep in his conversation, but he knows that this is a dinner party and conversation is supposed to change its tracks during the journey and go in another direction, so he remains silent for the moment to see which direction The Elvis steers the discussion express.

"It's basically a Celebrity Fuck List!" The Elvis scoffed snorting with laughter like a snuffling pig.

"What?" sneers The Host, obviously not happy with where this is going, but before he can intervene The Jesus nods, excitedly, in agreement.

"Fuck yeah!" he squeals excitedly "I've got one of those!" The Host's head swivels quickly, scowling at The Jesus.

"Wait just one second!" yells The Host, his voice raising to be heard over the snorting and scoffing of the two chauvinistic pigs.

"Jesus? Stay in fucking character!" his tone peppered with annoyance, again that unseen side of him rearing its ugly head. The goofy looking smile disappears from the face of The Jesus and is left resembling a naughty schoolboy who has been told off by his teacher.

"I don't think the 'Son of God' would have a celebrity fuck list!" Seethes The Hosts.

"Sorry!" comes the meek reply as The Jesus sinks down into his seat.

The Groucho shovels spoonful after spoonful of soup into his mouth annoyingly slurping as he demolishes the contents of the bowl that has already started to dribble down his chin, and in character squeaks "If this is Duck Soup, then where are the quackers?"

The table all look at him in awe of such a sight, he looks up, with soup dripping from his moustache and replies with wit as dry as a bone "Whatever it is, I'm against it!" and then carries on eating his soup.

There is a moment of silence before short bursts of sniggers take over the guests as well as The Host who finds this very amusing, obviously The Groucho Marx was added to his fantasy dinner party for a reason, his quirky one liners are thing of legend. But whether it was purposely done by The Groucho to diffuse the situation or not remains a mystery, but it did just that.

"So, are these celebrities alive or dead?" Asks The Groucho, interrupting the sniggering. "I mean I'd screw in a lightbulb but not in a corpse."

The Host looks on at The Groucho, his eyes rolling in annoyance, believing they had put this conversation behind them.

The Marilyn sits with her face frozen in contempt and horror at The Groucho's table manners.

"Gross!" The Marilyn scoffs.

The Groucho looks over at The Marilyn and winks, licking the droplets of soups that hang like icicles from his thick lips.

"Pig!" sneers The Marilyn.

"One morning I shot a pig in my pyjamas. How he got into my pyjamas I'll never know!" comes The Groucho's quick retort.

"Not necessarily!" Intervenes The Adolf, breaking his silence.

The Host's head turns quickly again, this time to face Adolf, "Adolf, in German if you please! Remember?" The Adolf nods in agreement and The Host's stern face contorts and a smile caresses his lips.

"Tut Mir Leid! Nicht unbedingt." (I'm Sorry! Not necessarily.)

The Groucho takes another slurp of wine and looks at The Adolf with one thick black eyebrow raised, like a wriggling caterpillar making its way across the creases of his forehead, "What did Frank say to the Furter?"

"He said, Not necessarily." Interrupts The Elvis. The Marilyn turns to The Elvis, looking at him very impressed.

"You speak German?" she asks.

"A little, I studied it at college. I wanted to become an interpreter and travel the world!" he replies. The two suddenly sink into their own conversation like no one else is in the room, there is a connection between the two. At first maybe it was just sexual, an attraction between two beautiful people, but now they seem to connect on an intellectual level.

"So, what do you do?" she asks.

The Elvis takes a swig of wine and then answers "I'm a mechanic."

"Didn't quite work out how you planned it then?" The Marilyn laughs.

"I guess not!" The Elvis smiles, shaking his head. The two of them just look at each other and laugh, until The Host bangs his fists down hard on the table. The sound of trembling cutlery shaking like petrified children under the impact and waves of wine rise up and out of glasses instantly staining the sleek white cotton table cloth with spots of ever expanding droplets of darkest red. He then presses the palms of his hands on the table and levers himself up to his feet. The room falls quiet and again his darker side is exhibited and doesn't fail to get everyone's attention again. He leans forward on the table as his face glows like the contents of a blood orange. Veins protrude from his forehead like convulsing mealworms trying to force their way out of his temples.

"Shut Up!" he yells.

There is complete silence and The Elvis and The Marilyn look up at The Host in shock.

"For Christ's sake, shut up!" he yells again.

The Jesus lowers the spoonful of soup that he is about to put into his mouth and looks at The Host with a bemused expression, "What did I do?"

The Host turns to The Jesus, cutting him a look that could burrow a hole into his soul. The Jesus' eyes grow wide, seemingly terrified, something in his eyes, no, behind his eyes, something dark locked away behind The Host's eyes. The Jesus slips the spoon into his mouth and lowers his head, sheepishly, as he refrains from making eye contact with The Host.

"Tonight, is not about what you do for a living, nor is it about what celebrities you would like to fornicate with!" The Host gently sinks back into his seat and rubs his temples slowly massaging and forcing the mealworms to slowly burrow back into his skull. He sighs heavily, his demeanour changes back again, he seems to have more sides than a Rubix cube.

"Although!" he speaks again, in that soft almost hypnotising voice, "Now I find myself very intrigued who these famous figures that sit in front of me would've like to have had sex with." The Host takes a sip of his wine and leans back into his chair again. His face returns to its original olive complexion and he no longer appears flustered.

"So, please do me the pleasure of quenching my curiosity!" says The Host, a wry smile caresses his lips.

The Groucho looks up from his rapidly emptying bowl and quips, "I remember the first time I had sex, I kept the receipt."

"Ah ist kommen auf die Welt offen! Es gibt so viele, dass Sie wahlen konnen!" (Ah, come on! The world is your oyster!

There are so many that you can choose from!) Smiles The Adolf with a perverse look on his face.

"Like?" asks the intrigued host.

"Nun gibt es Hepburn. Ich war schon immer eine Vorliebe für, Hepburn!" (Well, there's Hepburn. I've always been partial to Hepburn!) Said The Adolf with an uncharacteristically faraway look in his eye, daydreaming almost.

"How about that hot chick from Jersey Shore?" Says The Elvis, almost lustfully lost in a moments erotic fantasy of him grasping at her silicone implanted breast and suckling at her tough protruding nipples.

"Damn that girl is hot!" he says licking his lips.

"She got her looks from her Father. He's a plastic surgeon!" adds The Groucho.

"What's her name?" Enquires The Marilyn

"No idea!" shrugs The Elvis.

"Hmmm, maybe someone more from your own era, 'Elvis'?" says The Host, trying to keep him in character.

"Oh yeah, sure! Let me think." Replied The Elvis.

"There are quite a few to choose from. There were some beautiful women in your era, Elvis!" adds The Jesus.
The Marilyn looks on a little bemused, is she staying in character or is this who she would like under the platinum wig and beauty spot? "Maybe we could just tell you who we would like to do in real life?" She complained.
The Host shoots The Marilyn an irritated look in her direction.

"Why would I want to know that?" sneers The Host "I do not wish to know anything about your real lives! That would humanise you and ruin this whole experience for me. So, we will say only one person that you would fuck and not a list of five or else we'll be here all night! So, please, within the context of your characters, who would you erm... fuck?" Again, The Host's persona is showing more ups and downs than a roller coaster.

"Elvis? Have you had time to think?" asks The Host, returning once more to a soft voice.

"Doris Day!" says The Elvis.

"Very nice choice!" smiles The Host, excitedly nodding in agreement.

"Oh, she was so beautiful!" agrees The Marilyn.

"Is that your pick Marilyn?" Sniggered The Jesus, his eyes widening like a horny teenager.

"No!" laughs Marilyn "I'm not that way inclined."

"I for one would love to see you inclined that way, or even reclined!" says The Groucho, his thick black eyebrows wriggling up and down again vigorously like the wings of a butterfly.

"How about you Groucho?" The Host asks "So, who would it be?"

Groucho looks at him and places his spoon down into the remains of his soup, he wipes his mouth and soup caked moustache with his napkin and places the chunky cigar back into his mouth and flicks at his lighter. It's almost as though you can see the cogs in his head turning as he dissects the question. A small flame bursts from the silver plated lighter and wobbles there on the spot gyrating like an exotic belly dancer. The Groucho has the undivided attention of everyone around the

23

table and they await his answer with bated breath. Then with the cigar filling up the majority of his mouth, he suckles on it like a feeding new born and with smoke escaping from the corner of his mouth he speaks.

"I think women are sexy when they've got some clothes on. And if later they take them off then you've triumphed. Somebody once said it's what you don't see you're interested in, and this is true."

"Very poetically put, Groucho!" Says The Host.

"Die Frage antwortet aber nicht!" (Doesn't answer the question though!) Scoffs The Adolf.

"He's right, Groucho." agrees The Elvis "You kind of ducked the question there."

"Well, those are my principles, and if you don't like them... well, I have others!" chortles The Groucho winking at The Elvis. The table erupts in laughter and The Groucho stands up and takes a bow.

"I thank you, I thank you!"

"Jesus, you're up next." Says The Host smiling, still shaking his head at The Groucho's comment.

"Mary!" Answered The Jesus.
The Marilyn looks on in horror and disgust at The Jesus.

"Your Mother? That's just sick!" Growls the Marilyn, repulsed at his comment.
Jesus rolls his eyes at Marilyn.

"No! Of course not! I meant Mary Magdalene!" The Jesus snapped.
A bemused look caresses itself across The Marilyn's brow again.

24

"Who the fuck is Mary Magdalene?" she says.

Everyone freezes in time and stared at her as if she has just grown another head.

The Elvis feels bad for The Marilyn and attempts to break the silence and clue her in.

"She was..." starts The Elvis but is immediately cut off by The Host "Elvis, don't bother. You'll only confuse her."

The Host arrogantly dismissing that The Marilyn will understand. The Marilyn sticks her middle finger up at The Host which immediately brings a smirk to The Host's face. The Marilyn lights a cigarette and takes a drag on it before blowing smoke out of the corner of her plump red lips. The smoke rises and twirls around in the air and disperses around the chandelier.

"My apologies, Marilyn! What about you? What lucky guy would get the satisfaction of sleeping with Marilyn Monroe?" The Host tries to play nice as to not lose The Marilyn from his game.

"Well, that depends." The Marilyn is a little annoyed at being made the butt end of the joke, and the fact that she obviously doesn't understand, makes it worse. She feels stupid and she takes her time just to keep The Host waiting. It is obvious now that she does not care for him. She takes another drag on the cigarette, staining the white shaft of the cigarette pink from the pressure of her vibrant red lips.

"Do tell, Marilyn!" probes The Host.

She smirks, an answer settles on the back of her tongue and waits as she exhales yet more smoke into the air.

"Whoever's the president at the time!" Says The Marilyn, much to the pleasure of the table and laughter sweeps over everyone again.

"I'll do the jokes if you don't mind!" laughs The Groucho, wiggling his cigar between his fingers, and laughter explodes again.

"And last but not least, Adolf. How about you?" asks The Host, who is all smiles once again. The Adolf looks baffled.

"Wie zum Teufel wurde ich wissen, wer Adolf Hitler ficken wurde?" (How the hell would I know who Adolf Hitler would fuck?)

"Well, think!" replies the eager Host.

"Ich habe bereits erwähnt, hatte ich ein Faible für Audrey Hepburn?" (I did mention earlier I had a soft spot for Audrey Hepburn?) Answered The Adolf.

"Yes, but would she be able to straighten that swastika?" smirks The Groucho, gesturing with his right hand vigorously, simulating masturbation.

"Nun, denke ich, dass sie die Art scheint nicht. Es meiner Mutter war, die sowieso ein Fan von ihr war, verwendet habe ich nur, um ihre Filme zu sehen." (Well, I guess she doesn't seem the sort. It was my mom who was a fan of hers anyway, I just used to watch her movies.)

"Damn it, Adolf! We're not interested in your old dear's favourites from the silver screen!" Heckles The Host.

"Ich kann nicht jeder denken" (I can't think of anyone) pleads The Adolf, now feeling the pressure like a teenager in a schoolyard who is being egged on to do something stupid.

26

"Come on! I bet a guy like that, back in the day, with all that power, could have had his pick!" Probed The Elvis.

"Yeah, and with that cute little moustache, too!" The Marilyn winks and smiles as smokes exits her mouth again. The Adolf's eyes grow wide at just a small taste of The Marilyn's flirtatious manner. His cheeks blushing the colour of pickled beetroot as he quickly takes a swig of his wine to try and disguise the fact.

"So, who would it be Mein Fuhrer?" continues The Host. Adolf shrugs his shoulders and nonchalantly answers. "Die Juden!" (The Jews!)

The Host and Elvis burst out laughing, the others not understanding German, do not get the joke.

"What did he say?" asks The Marilyn

The Host is hysterical with laughter, so much so that tears well up in his eyes and balance ever so carefully on his lower eyelids. Finally, he manages to say, "The Jews!"

"Ja, ich die Juden einmal vor gefickt" (Yeah, I fucked the Jews once before.) The Adolf announces as he leans back in triumph sipping his wine.

"Hey J.C aren't you the King of the Jews?" asks The Groucho through his own sniggers.

"Yeah!" replies The Jesus, a smirk caressing his lips as he knows what The Groucho is getting at.

"Best watch out for old Adolf, over there!" says The Elvis "He may be after 'a Hunk, a Hunk of Burning Love'!"

Laughter again flows through the guests.

27

"And, what about you?" Marilyn nods her head towards The Host.

"Me?" He answers wiping tears from his eyes.

"Yeah! Who would you fuck?" she says with emphasis on the word fuck, that seems to seductively roll off her tongue. This is something that is not missed by any of the full bloodied males sitting around the table. The laughter stops, and silence falls over the group. All of them feeling a stir in their loins as they replay The Marilyn saying the word fuck through their heads again and again on a constant perverted loop of arousal.

"C'mon, sugar?" she smiles "Tell us who you'd do!"
They all turn to face The Host now, all of them wanting to know what mysteries lie behind the wall that their enigmatic host has built.

"Jessica Rabbit!" he answers

"Ha! Me too!" laughs The Elvis "I wanna change my answer!" he adds as snickers again flow through the guests.

Chapter 1

The Invitation

The Host shuffles through the corridor towards the hallway of the old gothic house, struggling with a very large poster of Elvis Presley, encased in a glass frame. Its awkward shape makes it difficult for him to manoeuvre, holding it in his sweaty palms, his hands grasping for a comfortable position, finally settling like the hands on a clock at 5:55.

He mumbles obscenities as he carefully squeezes through the narrow corridor, narrowly missing the mahogany wood panel wall. Finally, he reaches the hall entrance way and stops to take a breather. A layer of sweat showing on his forehead glistening under the light from the majestic chandelier that hangs above his head, like some gigantic diamond earring. He places the poster down on the floor, and gently leans it up against the staircase's chunky newel post. He retrieves a handkerchief from his trouser pocket and dabs at his brow, before stuffing it back into his pocket. The Host looks down at his hands, and the sharp indentations that have been left behind from the glass frames unforgiving edge. He rubs his hands together; the redness subsides a little. And he prepares to pick it up once again. He picks it up, again favouring the same grip that served him so well bringing it from the kitchen to his current destination.

"Fucking clowns!" he spits "Fucking stupid retarded movers! Why would they think I would hang a 40" X 60" framed picture of The King's film debut in the fucking kitchen!" as he pivots towards the doors of the dining room, he notices the rental sign placard propped up next to the front door. A vibrant red sign from E.J Wilson Rentals staring back at him, the words 'Available for Short Term Lease' in bright white font.

"I'll have to make sure I remove that as well!" he says heading towards the dining room "But, first things first!"

He sidesteps like a beached crab around an oval shaped mahogany dining table, which is shrouded with a pristine white cotton tablecloth and dressed elegantly with the finest china and silvery cutlery all placed for a three-course meal. Struggling with the oversized poster he adjusts it in his hands and lifts it up towards the round headed nail that protrudes from the wall, after a few unsuccessful attempts which are accompanied by several obscenities, it drops into place.

"Finally!" he sighs, arranging it into the position he desires "Perfect!" he takes a step back, with his hands-on hips, and admires the rooms newest feature "The piece da resistance."

He turns to survey his table, he smiles with arrogance and pride, before his face quickly retorts with a suddenly ugly bolt of irritation furrowing his moist brow. The reason for his change in attitude is a dessert spoon slightly askew, deviating slightly from the others which are all set to attention like soldiers on parade.

"We can't have that, now can we?" he tuts sliding the spoon back into the position he so desires.

"There!" he says matter-of-factly, casting a beady eye over the rest of the table in case there is anything else he has missed, there isn't. He makes his way out of the dining room, straightening a pile of vinyl records situated next to the gramophone. He closes the doors to the dining room behind him and heads across the hallway grabbing the 'For Lease' placard from its place of rest and walks into the study.

Several shelves smother the walls, the majority filled with books. Some shelves remain empty and adjacent to them, sits boxes of overflowing books, waiting patiently until they too are placed into their new dwelling place. A single lamp on a sturdy desk struggles to illuminate the gloomy room, and again, the mahogany furniture and features dominate and adds to the room's gloominess. Two wingback leather armchairs sit across from each other as if they're two old friends casually holding a conversation of times gone by. The Host places the placard in the corner of the room, sliding it out of sight by the side of an old grandfather clock that loudly ticks away, the sound almost hypnotic.

The Host strides across the room to a wooden globe drinks decanter. He opens the globe to unveil several bottles of alcohol, Koloff brand Vodka, Hackenschmidt brand Whiskey, and Queen brand Sherry as well as several chunky glasses. He pours himself a generous amount of Whiskey into his glass and takes a sip before approaching the twin armchairs. He slides into one of them, the one that is in close vicinity to a table that homes a vintage 1940's British Bakelite telephone. A Wild Pegasus brand cigar box along with a glass cut ashtray, that looks like it has never been used for its purpose, not a trace of ash or residue, not even as much as a chip in the glass.

He inspects the 6 inch Cuban, rubbing his fingers up and down it as he looks for any imperfections, there are none. He holds it under his nose and takes in its organic leafy aroma. Satisfied with the cigar he prepares it, taking his silver plated cutter from the cigar box he removes the cap in one quick movement, letting it fall into the empty ashtray, like the head of an aristocrat falling to Madame guillotine in 18th Century's French Revolution.

The lighter (that matches the cutter, obviously purchased as a set) is ignited and warms the foot of the cigar until it starts to smoulder. He inhales the fresh goodness of the cigar and closes his eyes in a moment of joy, and suddenly the room is filled with the thick smoke of the Cuban encasing The Host in a cocoon. After several minutes enjoying his cigar and glass of whiskey, he places the glass down and his fingers pinch the cigar safely in place while he picks up the telephone receiver. With the cigar trapped between his middle and ring finger, he uses his index finger to dial the appropriate number sequence. He leans back in the chair, its leather singing to him with his every movement. Again he enjoys his Cuban as the phone rings out on the other end of his receiver.

In his ear the phone rings once, twice, three times.

He taps the excess ash forming into the ashtray, the burning embers falling like snow around the already discarded cap.

It rings for the fourth time.

Gently, he places the cigar into the ashtray, balancing on the groove that is cut into the lip of the glass for such an occasion. The smoke continues to float softly into the air.

Five times. Six times...

"Good Morning, 10 out of 10 Look-Alike Agency, Anna speaking. How can I help you today?" comes the enthusiastic voice of a female, the sound of her voice sounds young, maybe her first job since leaving college.

"Why, hello Anna! And how are you this morning?" he replies in his velvety tone, almost flirtatious but not offensive.

"Oh! I am fine, thank you Sir." A little taken aback by such a pleasant greeting (obviously not used to such treatment from customers, it's quite possible she is used to dealing with irate customers and their complaints) "How can I be of service?"

"Well, I am throwing a little shindig and I am looking for six lookalikes for a dinner party." He says matter-of-factly, looking smug and arrogant, which is lost on the young lady at 10 out 10 as she can't see this.

"Six!" She unprofessionally shrieks (Again obviously quite new to the job and her inexperience showing at such a large order). "Oh, I am sorry. I'm just not used to such a large quantity!"

"That's quite alright my dear! Is this too outrageous of a request? Can you help me?"

"Oh, yes, Certainly sir! When would you require our services?"

"Tomorrow night! At 21 hundred hours!"

"That is a little late notice, sir." She says, almost sad now, knowing that it may not be possible, and she would lose a hefty amount of commission if she can't make this happen.

The Host picks up his cigar and takes a drag, blowing smoke into the air. The smoke dances around him.

"Come now, I'm sure you can work your magic Anna!" he says, so charming, that she can't resist.

"I... I shall try, sir. But it won't be easy at such late notice."

"Tell them I will pay them all double!"

"Double!" She says shocked again unable to conceal her inexperience.

"Yes, double!"

"Certainly, Sir! Now who would you like for your dinner party?"

The Host takes another drag on the cigar and, again, blows smoke into the air. He taps more excess ash into the ashtray.

"Well, that's the fun part isn't it?"

CHAPTER 2

BOBBY

The small town at the foot of Blackfoot Ridge is usually quite quiet and quaint, but today a cacophonous cluster of metal on metal serenades the town of Little Blackfoot in the midday sunshine.

Under the cover of Dahlman's Auto Repair, a ramshackle garage built up mostly of corrugated sheets of metal, with a gradient of steel to rust. The sign has left its better days far behind now and struggles to advertise the business as the words have either fallen off, or started to merge with the heavily stained sign itself. The combination of severe weather and sheer lack of tender loving care has seriously done a number on it.

The battered roller door, like the structure itself is riddled with rust and damage, but in places there is the remnants of pealing blue paint from a forgotten time that continues to cling on to the surface. Inside through the sounds of spasmodic banging and revving of engines, the sounds of Radio Blackfoot fights to be heard under such a ruckus, which was currently playing the classic 'Lay Lady Lay' by Bob Dylan.

On the small forecourt stood three automobiles awaiting repair, sitting there patiently like people in a clinic's waiting room. The cars vary in style, brand and colour. An immaculate Cadillac El Dorado 1959 in a luscious scarlet trimmed in ivory to make its edges really stand out. With its convertible roof down, it exposes the white leather interior and dashboard as it takes in the sun's rays as if it's sunbathing.

A black broken-down 1949 Mercury 6 Passenger Coupe edged with a decaying rust trim, stands almost embarrassed next to the pristine Cadillac, oil dripping from underneath its chassis as if it were its tears.

The last vehicle that is located right in front of the garage doors is a worn 1951 Chevy truck in a cool midnight blue, the colour of those moonless night skies. The hood of the truck is up and the figure of a man in slate coloured overalls covered in petrol stains can be seen bent over, partially hidden by the shade of the hood as he works on the engine. His foot taps along with the gravelling tones of Dylan and he fluctuates from singing parts of the song to whistling along with the tune. Somewhere inside the garage a bell rings. A high pitch harpies wail stings the ears of anyone in the vicinity. It screeches through the sounds of thumping of hammers, the dropping of wrenches, the coughing of engines, the slamming of doors, the rumbling of a generator and unfortunately it all but drowns out Dylan's 1969 hit.

"Pa! Phone!" Shouts the mechanic that is still halfway inside the Chevy's gapping hood, from a distance it looks like some prehistoric creature devouring the poor man.

The bell continues to constantly ring.

"Pa!" he calls again, louder this time, even making his own ears ring from the velocity of his voice as it ricochets off the hood "Deaf old buzzard" he adds mumbling under his breath this time.

"I got it, I got it!" comes the hoarse reply as an old man dressed in the same slate coloured overalls as his son working on the Chevy, passes by the entrance inside the garage, rubbing his hands on a red cloth as he disappears out of sight.

Suddenly the ringing stops, abruptly and all that can now be heard is Dylan's gruffness filling the garage. Moments later, the old man exits the garage and shuffles towards the Chevy. The wriggling backside of the mechanic gyrates rhythmically to the song.

"Bobby!" says the man through a spluttering cough which he then covers with his oil stain red cloth.

"Yeah, Pa?" Bobby says popping his head out of the concealment of the Chevy's hood, his eyes squinting in the sunlight.

"That lady at the agency is on the phone again!"

"I told her I couldn't work this weekend!" Bobby sighs.

"Don't shoot the messenger, kid." Says his father, turning around with his hands in the air as he heads back into the garage.

Bobby wipes his handsome moist brow with a cloth of his own before stuffing it into the sagging rear pocket of his overall.

"Goddamn it! I've got three cars to finish by Monday and I promised I'd take Ann Marie out tomorrow night!"

His groaning falls on deaf ears as the figure of his father shrugs and disappears inside.

"Fuck!" he sighs wiping his oil stained face with the palm of his hand.

He walks with purpose towards the inside of the garage, his jet black hair caressed back, containing about as much oil as the Chevy, glistens in the sun and two sharp sideburns meet his stubbled square jaw.

"I'll say, 'look I don't want to let you down, but I already have plans', hey you're not lying! You shouldn't feel guilty! Shit just tell 'em!"

He walks towards the telephone that is fixed on the office wall, covered in oil stains and next to a calendar of nudes, the month set to May and the pinup is the infamous Barbie Butkus kneeling over a picnic basket wearing nothing but her goosebumps.

"Hey, this is Bobby... Yeah, I know but I'm really busy at the moment and I have plans for...double!... For real? I'll be there."

Chapter 12

Why Us?

With the soup going down a storm and the sound of sniggers starting to die down, the sound of slurping fills the room once again.

The Marilyn daintily sips her soup as ladylike as possible, the greenish tone of the soup being absorbed by the plump red of her lips. She stops and lowers her spoon, licking her lips her face appearing placid as she looks lost in thought.

The Host notices and interrupts her musing.

"Is there something wrong, my dear Marilyn?" She snaps out of it and replies with a "huh?"

"Your soup possibly? Is there something not to your liking?"

"Oh! Oh no! No, not at all! The soup is great. I was just thinking."

"Please enlighten us!" The Host asks smiling, whilst dabbing away the soup from his mouth with his napkin.

"I was actually just thinking, why us?" She looks around at the rest of the guests gathered at the table. To an onlooker it would look like some obscure scene from a Madame Tussauds exhibit.

"That is an excellent question my dear!" The Host answers and claps his hands together with excitement.
The guests all stop the scooping of soup for a moment and turn their attention to The Host, who leans back in his chair, clasping his hands together.

"Well, I have thrown many a dinner party over the years, some of them you could say were social experiments, I guess. This one is no different."

"So, we are the guinea pigs?" The Elvis asks.

"Yes, I guess you could say that!" Chuckles The Host.

"Charming!" Laughs The Groucho

"As I said, I have thrown many a party, most of them having themes, usually. You know Halloween, Toga or Murder Mystery evenings. All of them are most fun, but this time I wanted to do something a little different."

"Do you always invite strangers to these gatherings?" Asks The Jesus.

"Yes. Well, most of the time. It helps for my experiments to have people I don't know. I guess that when you socialise with your friends and family, you have heard all the stories before and some of the conversation can become forced as they know what you like and what you don't like, so they can manipulate the conversation to fit that. This way it's totally new conversations, opinions and stories. And adding to that you are all playing characters which adds another layer to it that makes it more exciting for all of us. Don't you think?"

The heads around the table all nod in agreeing unison.

"Aber warum diese bestimmte Auswahl von Menschen?" (But why this particular selection of people?) asks The Adolf.

"It's probably down to personal taste. But I asked myself who were the most iconic people throughout history to me. And to me you people gathered around this table tonight are just that."

"You know I think you are the most intellectual man I have ever met." The Groucho states shaking his head in disbelief.

"Really?" Laughs The Host.

"No, but I don't mind lying if it gets me a second helping!" The Groucho smiles. Laughter rises.

CHAPTER 3

FLOYD

There are 5,316 franchises of the horror themed fast food restaurant, Franken-Burger, across North America. The branch that is situated in Studd City happens to be a newly opened establishment and on this beautiful sunny afternoon, business is booming.

A steady stream of cars snake through the drive-through, bumper to bumper like the shackled trucks of a train, some impatient customers take their frustrations out on their horns, the service obviously not living up to the moniker of 'fast' food.

A gangly looking guy clad in a uniform of green and red, shuffles around the outdoor seating area and collects litter with a claw grabber and stuffs it unenthusiastically into a trash bag. Behind him the medieval haunted castle theme of the building shades him from the sun, the logo flashes with a jade tinted electrical current flashing the word 'Franken' sitting between two conductor bolts that protrude from the gaps of a gigantic hamburger that is stitched together like the limbs of Frankenstein's Monster himself, the word 'Burger' is etched on the base of the sign. The young man looks around suspiciously, his cratered complexion from years of abuse from that pubescent bully known as acne wrinkles as his eyes turn to slits. He approaches a bench where a pile of leftover debris has been left, a piece of burger remains in its container. Unfinished, complete with toothmarks sunk into the bun and meat, the tiniest bit of lettuce hangs out from between it, sandwiched in tightly. He looks around again, hoping that nobody is looking at him, and as he is dragging the packets and wrappers into his trash bag, he slides the piece of unfinished burger into his mouth and quickly gnaws on it.

"Say one thing about them, they make an awesome fucking burger!"

He picks up what he thinks is an empty soda cup, but there is a little of pineapple Koko Soda sloshing around in the shards of ice that haven't yet melted. Again, he looks around and with coast all clear he slurps up the remaining drink up through a straw that disgustingly has a flat end where it has been nibbled by its previous consumer. This doesn't faze him, and he empties it until all that is heard is the annoying sound of the sucking up of the plastic. He discards the empty cup into the trash bag and stands looking out to the busy city and the queue at the drive through getting longer, all slowly chugging their way around the restaurant. He scratches at his hair, a mass of it curled up into an uncomfortable hairnet, which sits underneath a Frankenstein's Monster themed flattop hat, that is complete with protruding bolts. He looks around and focuses in on a flock of stubby legged cooing pigeons, all pecking away at a box of fries that had somehow found its way onto the floor of the car park. He licks his lips and approaches the scene unbeknownst to the pigeons.

"Back off vermin. This is my turf!" he seethes waving his grabbing claw at them "Get out of here! Go on!" he shouts. The pigeons flee reluctantly leaving behind the heavily salted goodness behind.

He scoops up a handful fries and attempts to stuff them into his waiting gape.

"Floyd!" comes an annoyed cry from the entrance of the restaurant. He drops the fries and spins on the spot to face the entrance. The restaurants shift manager stands hands on his hips looking very annoyed at Floyd.

"I wasn't doing anything!" Floyd spits.

"I know you aren't! You never seem to do anything!" he seethes, shaking his head in distain. Luckily his manager didn't see him trying to eat the leftovers or he would have surely been fired.

"I'm just collecting the trash like you asked, Mr Holden."

"Floyd, that was over an hour ago!" he sighs "What the hell have you been doing out here?"

"Nothing!" he murmurs, his answer riddled with guilt.

"Well, that I can believe! C'mon inside we're getting busy and I need you on the register."

"What about this stuff?" Floyd says, staring at the leftover fries scattered on the floor like a game of pick up sticks.

"Just leave them for the pigeons." Says his manager before walking back into the restaurant.

"Fucking Pigeons!" Floyd murmurs as he casually drops his trash bag and claw, before shuffling after him with all the urgency of some flesh eating zombie.

The restaurant that is decorated throughout with red and green striped interior and furnishings is heaving. Several queues of people, the majority of them look pissed off with the amount of time they have been waiting, but mostly the place is filled with family conversations and the happy giggling of children enjoying their monster themed food.

The manager ushers Floyd behind the counter where the two other cashiers look flustered and just as annoyed as some of the customers. Frankenstein's Monster latex scalps sitting on their heads askew from constant bouncing around as they collect orders for customers.

"Do you know what gifts are available in this week's Fright Fest for the kids?" asks his manager who keys in the correct code to enable Floyd to sign in.

"Erm, nope!" Answers Floyd, The manager's eyes roll backwards as if he's trying to get a glimpse at his own scalp.

"This week it has a cardboard Frankenstein hat, Dracula fangs and cape, and a spider ring."

"Frankenstein hat?"

"Yeah, Frankenstein hat."

"You do know he's not called Frankenstein?"

"What?" The manager looks at him confused

"What're you talking about?"

"The Monster! He's not actually called Frankenstein." shrugs Floyd nonchalantly.

"So, what's his name then? Clive?" The manager snaps back with sarcasm.

"He didn't have a name." Floyd shrugs again before adding "It's like a very common misconception that he's Frankenstein, something that has gotten lost in translation over the years. Frankenstein was the name of the doctor, not the monster."

The manager stares at him, his first thought probably being 'what has this guy been smoking' before dismissing what he has just said by reiterating what is available in the Fright Fest again "As I was saying... Cape, Fangs, Ring and a Frankenstein's... 'Monster' hat!"

"Okay." Floyd says again shrugging, with little to know enthusiasm.

"Can you remember how to work the register?"

"Yeah, sure!" Again comes the shrug that is rapidly becoming a trait.

"Hop on then. I'll stay right here, and we'll see how you do."

Floyd stands at the register and scratches at his beard looking totally disinterested.

"Don't scratch your beard, Floyd! It's not hygienic. Remind me to find you a beard net!" says The manager passing him some hand sanitiser that he squirts onto his hand and rubs it in vigorously.

"Next!" Floyd wails in such a tired monotone voice.

A middle aged male customer approaches the register, gazing up at the menu above them.

"Welcome to Franken-Burger where we sell fiendishly fun fast food. What ghoulish combination of terrifyingly tasty refreshments can I get you?" he asks in such a dull uninterested voice that the manager just drops his head and rubs his eyes, he knows he may well be fighting a losing battle.

"Yeah, can I get a Monster Burger with everything on it?" the customer asks.

Floyd pushes a button on the electronic cash register in front of him. As he pushes the button, it is accompanied by a beep, it should be noted that the other cashiers' registers are erupting with a plethora of beeps, indicating they are both indeed faster and more efficient at their jobs than Floyd.

"Would you like a side order of Frightful Franken-Fries with that?"

"Sure! Why not! Large please."

Floyd slowly pushes another button and, pecking at it with his bony finger like a bird in search of an earthworm.

"And what about a blood curdling beverage?"

The customer shakes his head as he retrieves his wallet and flits through his dollar bills "No, thanks."

"Oh, but if you have the blood curdling beverage then it qualifies as a Transylvanian Nightmare Combo and you can save 60 cents off your order." This pitch to try and add on to the sale could not have been more horrible or ungenuine and his manager actually face palms himself. But amazingly it worked, and the customer said, "Okay, sure. What have you got?"

"Koko pop in an array of flavours. Putrid Pineapple, Revolting Raspberry, Slime Lime, Vamp-ade, Creepy Cola and oh!... Orange."

"I'll take a regular Vamp-ade." and holds out the bills to pay for his meal.

"That will be $6, please." Floyd answers with almost a sigh.

Floyd saunters off to collect the customer's order.

The manager turns his attentions to a female member of staff busy wiping over tables "Jess?" he calls, she turns to him in mid wipe "Yeah?"

"Can you serve behind the counter please. I need to chat with Floyd."

"Sure!" she answers pleasantly and quickly moves into position behind the register, rapidly inputting her number to use it. Floyd arrives back and hands over the Transylvanian Nightmare Combo to the customer who leaves while Floyd drones out the final part of his service routine.

"Thank you for stopping by at Franken-Burger. Have a dastardly day!"

Jess takes over at the cash register and Floyd shuffles over towards the manager who stands near the wall out of the way of all the rushing around staff members. Floyd drives his index finger up his nostril and it

squirms around inside with reckless abandon.

"Floyd!" The manager yelps.

"Yeah?" comes the casual answer from Floyd, finger still stood fast up his nose. The manager pulls him closer and lowers his voice. "What have I told you about picking your nose?"

"Not to do it?"

"Exactly! So, stop it!"

Floyd slowly takes his finger out of his nose and wipes the mucus on his shirt.

The manager rubs his eyes again and sighs heavily "I've been keeping a close eye on you, Floyd, and your customer service is unacceptable!"

Floyd looks at the manager like he is in a daze, not really listening to what his boss is saying.

"I've just watched you serve that gentleman and I was appalled with your attitude. If you want to get a golden bat on that badge, Floyd, you'll have to buck your ideas up. Are you even listening to what I am saying?" he adds.

Floyd nods at him. The manager leans in closer, looking at him through squinting suspicious eyes.

"Have you been smoking that shit again on your break?"

Floyd shakes his head slowly.

"You better not have been! Here at Franken- Burger we do not condone drug use! Do you understand?"

"Yeah!" Floyd shrugs.

The manager leans in ever closer and whispers in his ear.

"Look, Floyd, I know I'm dating your mom and I said I'd get you a job, but if you keep fucking up, I'm going to have to let you go!"

"Okay, Jim." Floyd whispers back "Do you want me to carry on picking up the litter?"

The manager sighs and just gives in with the lifeless answer "Yeah!"

The phone hanging on the wall next to them rings a droning high pitch tone and makes the manager jump.

"This is Franken-Burger, we serve Fiendishly Fun Fast Food to terrorise your tastebuds. This is Jim speaking how can I help?" there is a pause and he sighs again "Floyd. It's for you!" he says handing him the receiver.

CHAPTER 13

BURNING, FRESHLY CUT GRASS AND THERE SMELLS

"Freshly cut grass!" The Jesus says softly, his eyes almost closed shut as he mused through memories of his favourite smell.

"Oh, yeah, that's a good one!" Marilyn agrees, the table nod in agreement.

"Yep, there's not a lot of things in this world that smell as good as when Pa would cut the lawn." The Elvis reminisces with a smile on his face, a faraway look in his eye lost in this moment with that smirk on his face he looks the spitting image of the king himself. It is with facials like this that you can see why he has
the job.

"I can see the old buzzard now, breaking his back trying to push that medieval looking lawnmower across the grass. Stopping to wipe the sweat from his brow and stretch out his aching bones..."

"So eine schöne Erinnerung!" (Such a beautiful memory!) Smiles The Adolf, even him as lookalike doesn't look right with a smile. It seems alien sitting on his face, curling up either end around that square of moustache.

"Isn't it just?" The Elvis smiles "He's a great guy my Pa." The host's eyes widen, and his veins start to squirm either side of his temples, but The Elvis realises his mistake as his real life had out boxed his character's.

"WAS!" he quickly intervenes before The Host can unleash yet more venom "He was a great guy" he then smiles at The Host; whose face contorts back to normal and he smiles back.

"Yes, poor old Vernon!" The Host nods.

"Freshly pumped gas for me!" says Marilyn lighting up another cigarette, pressing it between her moist red lips and blowing smoke out of the corner of her pursed mouth, "Yeah, that's a sexy smell. Really clogs up your nostrils don't you think?"

They nod in agreement, all apart from The Jesus whose face contorts, as if he wears the mask of someone about to vomit, his stomach knots like a wet towel being rung out, "Oh, no! I can't stand the smell of gasoline. Really turns my stomach."

"And then there's of course the smell of a freshly lit Cavalier!" she holds the cigarette out in front of her face and inhales the smoke, it dances around her pale narrow nostrils before disappearing up her nasal passage. The whole table watches in complete silence again, hypnotised by her sexual appeal and charm, much like the real Marilyn.

"Inhale! Feel that mildness - taste that flavour - that's a Cavalier!" recalling an ad campaign for the particular brand back in 1954.

"Now, I like the smell of burning!" says The Groucho who had been biding his time and waiting for the opportune moment to hit the gathering with yet another witty punchline "I used to love toasting marshmallows at the crematorium, yeah, being a scout leader was fun."

The table erupts with laughter again, and The Groucho laps up the adulation of the room.

"But in all seriousness..." He says bringing his audience back down "I wish to be cremated!" even having some of them look at him through furrowed brows of seriousness and concern. He has them in the palm of his hand, much like the quick witted individual he is now portraying, "One tenth of my ashes shall be given to my agent... as written in our contract!"

Chapter 14

Tell Me A Story

With the conversation flowing nicely now and everyone seemingly at ease with their surroundings, The Host looks to stir the pot and steer the conversation again.

"What if I asked you all to tell me a story?" The Host announces.

The guests look at him and all move a little uneasily in their seats. None of them want to do anything that would make them appear foolish.

"What d'you mean?" asks The Elvis.

"Exactly what I said. Tell me a story!"

"About what?" The Marilyn chimes in, looking somewhat bemused again.

"Oh, it can be about anything really. I don't mind."

The guests look at each other all of them bewildered.

"Oh, I don't know any stories!" moaned The Jesus.

The Host cuts him a look that was so cold it could have been an icicle being pierced into his face.

"Erm, maybe I'd better leave?" The Jesus gulps.

"You can leave in a huff. Or you can leave in a minute and a huff!" quips The Groucho.

The Host's face changes again, like some chameleon and he smiles, "Don't be silly, Jesus. You sit right there." He leans back into his chair again "I don't want you all to over think this and think that I'm going to make you perform or anything. Just tell me story. A tale you have heard or an experience you have had. Just a nice little anecdote"

He waits.

"Ich kenne eine Geschichte." (I know a story.) Announced The Adolf, realising that no one else was going to get the ball rolling.

"Oh, wonderful!" squawks The Host "Please do go on."

All the eyes turn to look at The Adolf and his Adam's apple forces its way down past his tight shirt collar and then rises back. He suddenly felt like a child at school again and could feel all the eyes burning into him, so much that he thought he was going to melt into a puddle. He takes a deep breath and begins.

"Es ist berechtigt, Joseph." (It is entitled, Joseph.) Immediately The Elvis started to translate into English for all the non-German speaking guests. Both The Host and The Adolf appreciated this and they let him know with a nod of their heads. The Adolf dived straight in and started to tell the story…

JOSEPH

Der Name ist Joseph, aber sie nennen mich Joey. Ein Lebenslänglich, jawohl, um zu sagen, dass ich niemals hier rauskomme und das ist Gottes ehrliche Wahrheit. Ich weiß nicht wirklich, wie lange ich hier eingesperrt bin, um ganz ehrlich zu dir zu sein, es ist eine lange Zeit, obwohl ich dir das sagen kann.

Ich hätte hier ein Stückchen kratzen können, aber sie mögen das nicht, und ich möchte keine Federn ruinieren, halte einfach den Kopf gesenkt. Ich mag diese Tage keine Aufregung.

Ich erinnere mich an eine Weile zurück, muss jetzt Jahre sein, aber wer kann sagen, ich war viel jünger und dumm, ich denke, Angst ist das beste Wort, ja, ich hatte Angst. In der ersten Nacht, in der sie mich hierher gebracht haben, habe ich eine kleine Klappe geschlagen, oh, die Hitzigkeit der Jugend. Mir wurde nicht gesagt, was ich tun sollte, was ich essen konnte, wenn ich schlafen konnte, nein, mein Herr, und als sie mich in diese Zelle brachten, schlug ich aus. Einen von ihnen ziemlich gut zu schneiden, sicher Blut zu ziehen, aber ich wurde im Nahkampf zu Boden geworfen und meine Köpfe fühlten sich seither nie mehr so an. Es war alles sehr psychisch störend und ich verbrachte die ganze Nacht wach und dachte, dass ich für den Rest meiner Tage nicht so leben könnte. Ich musste das Beste aus dieser Situation machen.

Also, fing ich an, die positiven Dinge zu sehen, versuchte es trotzdem, ich wurde jeden Tag gefüttert und getränkt, jeden Tag mit der gleichen Scheiße, aber es könnte schlimmer sein und sie gaben mir freundlicherweise die Materialien, die ich für meine

Bildhauerei brauchte Ich kann beim Schnitzen viel Aggression herauslassen, das ist sehr therapeutisch für mich. Was ich erschaffe, sieht vielleicht für niemanden anders aus, aber für mich ist es kreativer Ausdruck.

Um ehrlich zu sein, die Zelle selbst ist recht geräumig, ich meine, der letzte Ort, an dem ich war. Ich war dort mit sechs zu einer Zelle gepackt. Ich meine, du stellst dir vor, ein wenig Privatsphäre unter dieser Menge zu bekommen ohne dass einer ihrer Knopfaugen mich anstarrte. Hat viele Kämpfe verursacht, die ich dir erzählen kann. Ich schätze, ich habe das Glück, dass ich diesen ganzen Raum für mich habe. Sie haben versucht, mir einen Mitbewohner zu geben, was mir nichts ausgemacht hat, wie heißt er jetzt? Pete ... nein, nein, ich habe Unrecht, es war Percy, es war lange her und mein Verstand ist nicht so wie er war. Aber ja, Percy war in Ordnung, nicht viel von einem Gesprächspartner, aber es war in Ordnung, wie ich sagte, es gibt genug Platz, um hier zu teilen. Nun, eine Nacht war Percy krank, wirklich krank, sein Kopf schaukelte heftig vor und zurück und er warf sich überall hoch, der Gestank war schrecklich. Nun, Percy ist irgendwie gestorben, hat sich zusammengerollt und ist gestorben. Er liegt dort in einer Pfütze seines eigenen Erbrochenen. Ich musste die ganze Nacht mit dem armen Percy verbringen, Dead.

Ich habe versucht, sie dazu zu bringen, mich zu hören, aber das haben sie nicht getan und erst am Morgen haben sie ihn gefunden und seinen Kadaver herausgenommen. Der Gestank von Tod und Krankheit dauerte noch eine Ewigkeit.

Ja, die Dinge könnten definitiv schlimmer sein. Es gibt nichts anderes zu tun, als mich selbst im Spiegel zu betrachten, was keinen Spaß macht, wenn man in mein Alter kommt, man bemerkt jeden Makel, es wird so deprimierend. Manchmal höre ich den Klang von Musik, die irgendwo herkommt, nicht zu weit weg, eine Zelle in meinem Block hat ein Radio und ich frage, warum haben sie eins und ich nicht? Aber wenn du auf die Kräfte schießt, die du sein wirst, wirst du nicht belohnt werden, bist du. Was mache ich jetzt? Wahrscheinlich sitze ich nur für den Rest des Tages hier oder vielleicht setze ich mich dort hin, es wird heller und es ist wärmer, wenn die Sonne scheint, aber da saß Percy, also ist es ein bisschen deplatziert.

Ich denke, es ist Mittag, da die Sonne jetzt hier blendet, warm aber warm und schön, ich kann meine Augen schließen und eine Weile in ihrem Glanz ruhen.

Fünf Minuten später fiel Joey von seiner Stange. Tot.

* For English translation please see page 157

They all start laughing.

"Oh, that was so very clever. Bravo, Adolf, bravo!" applauds The Host.

"Vielen Dank" (Thank you)

"That was so much fun, Honey!" winks The Marilyn.

The Adolf soaks up the adulation, proud but slightly embarrassed, his cheeks blemished with a tint of plum.

"Groucho! You go next!" Chuckles The Host.

The Groucho looks at him blank, he looks like he's going to break character, suddenly out of his comfort zone.

"You must know a story, surely?" demands The Host, his patience starting to waver now, and the rest of the guests can feel it and they stop laughing and look at The Groucho.

"I...erm..." The Grouch murmurs quietly.

"Come on!" probes The Host.

"How about a joke?" The Elvis intervenes, trying to defuse the situation.

"Yeah, tell us a joke, Honey!" adds The Marilyn. "Very well!" concedes The Host.

"Now jokes I've got in heaps!" The Groucho smiles, straight back into character.

"Did you hear about the pregnant bed bug?" He asks and is met by numerous shakings of heads. "It's having a baby in the spring!" and then he wags the cigar between his fingers while elevating his chunky thick eyebrows.

There is a drone throughout the room and then some stifled laughter, just because of how bad the joke was. The host quickly turns to The Marilyn and doesn't even acknowledge The Groucho's sad attempt.

"What about you, Marilyn? Surely you have some tales to tell?"

"I have tales, but I don't think any of them are fit for dinner party conversation!" she smirks.

"Now you have our attention!" The Jesus salivates.

"No, I can't! The one that has popped into my head is too gross and way too embarrassing."

"Oh, this one is a real story?" The Elvis asks

"Yeah! But it's really sick and... Oh. No, I don't want to tell it."

"C'mon my dear, Marilyn! We are all friends here!" The Host says smiling at her.

"It's sick!" she whines.

"The sicker the better my dear!" The Host stares at her with perverted eyes.

She looks around and those same eyes are seen in the other guests.

They want me to tell them something dirty! Something sordid and sexual! The dirty fucking perverts. I'll lure them in and hit them with a punchline that would floor a heavyweight.

The Marilyn smiles sadistically, and licks her lips, her moist tongue causing her lipstick to shine "Okay. You asked for it!"

The gathering lean in as to hear every word from those luscious lips of hers.

"I've had a lot of guys in my time. I mean a lot! And sometimes I come across some certain types that... how should I put it? Well, they like to be kinky and try things."

The guest's eyes grow and there is definite twitching between their legs.

She has them.

"Now, I am always game to try new sexual positions or fads. Bring it on I say!"

The loins of the guests tingle with excitement.

"So, when this guy came to me and said that he was into eproctophilia, I thought sure why not. Couldn't hurt right?" The Marilyn asked. She looked around the table and they were all looking at her, she knew that not one of them knew what eproctophilia was, if they did, they would surely not want her to continue her story. They all nod and agree with her, going along with whatever she says now.

"So, we took off our clothes and I pushed him gently onto the bed, then I do a little dance. I usually do a little dance just to make sure their little man is awake. Nothing to crazy, just pushing my breasts together, gyrating my pelvis in his face, rubbing my fingers over my pussy. Tempting him you know?" She is met by widened eyes and hanging jaws.

"I start to suck his dick. Slow at first and then lick it up and down. Not to forget his balls either!" There is a shuffling of feet below the table as the guests no doubt adjust their feet and legs to make way for the erections that have all simultaneously popped up.

"This guy is really eager for me to get straight down to what he likes and so he lies back on the bed. I crawl across the bed towards him and I straddled him, using his face as a saddle and I just rub myself all over his face. He wants me to do it, I can hear his muffled groans spilling out underneath me and he grabs my ass cheeks and squeezes them hard. I'd never done it before but it's what he wanted so I did it!" She says cutting the story short and then raises her glass to take a sip of her wine.
Silence.

61

"Then what happened?" The Host asks.

"What did you do to him?" The Jesus asks

"Was wollte er von dir?" (What did he want you to do?) The Adolf added.

All of them leaning forward, not a hand on the table could be seen now as they waited with bated breath.

"Why, I farted on him! What did you think I was going to do?" She giggles knowing she had them. Their faces immediately changed, and they sank back into their chairs. It was almost as if you could hear their erections deflating like punctured balloons.

"Yeah! That is what eproctophilia is. A fetish for smelling farts."

The faces of the guests look drained and no longer interested.

"But that is not all of the story!" she added.

Their ears prick up again and the thought that maybe the story will end on a better note.

"Unfortunately, I had been eating spicy food earlier on that day." She made a grimaced face and mimicked rubbing her stomach. "So, he kind of got a little more than he'd bargained for. I'm afraid I sharted!"

Everyone's face in the room turned a sickly green tint and they all looked on horrified.

"I think I'm gonna throw up!" says The Jesus.

"There are no words." The Groucho says shaking his head.

"Well, that definitely was a story!" The Host says dabbing his brow with his napkin.

"I can top that!" The Elvis declares and is met by a look of shock and disgust.

"There is no way you can top that, surely?" Says The Jesus in disbelief.

"You wanna bet?" The Elvis grinned "Now, just so we are straight, this story didn't happen to me, but..."

THE CUBICLE

"I really need a dump" John said as he made his way down the high street. He immediately got an odd look from an old lady shuffling past him on the sidewalk, her pink rinsed hair carefully protected from the breeze wrapped in a floral silk head scarf. The squeaky wheeled shopping trolley being dragged behind her, no doubt filled with the day's bargains in all the finest knickknack establishments that the town had to offer. It was a look of disgust more than anything, that's when John realised he'd said that out loud.

Whoops! He thought as he passed her wrinkled gurning face and hit back with an awkward slightly embarrassed smile.

His stomach gurgled. The contents of his bowels churning away like an over worked coffee percolator and sounding like one too.

Oh crap. I really need to get to the toilet. Sharpish!

He clutched his stomach and slowed his pace and shuffled along slowly for a moment until the cramping ceased.

Not here. Don't do it here!

He waited, stood perfectly still like a statue you'd see in a museum from ancient Greece.

63

Passers-by continued with the odd looks, but nobody daren't ask if he was okay, that would be too much to ask of today's society.

The cramping stopped, and John carried on.

Irritable Bowel Syndrome is a bitch. It really is. You know all those favourites you have? Sausages? Bacon? Kebabs? Curry? Yep you can count Old John out of all that and it's totally shit.

He looks in a shop window being stocked by a young pert female shop assistant. Her tight pencil skirt stretched around her perfectly peach-like bottom. She bends over to pick up some shoes.

Fucking hell! Look at that. He thought.

She turns around with her hands clutching several pairs of ladies' shoes. She was very pretty, and her long auburn hair hung either side of her face, as if it was framing her beauty.

Damn, she is hot. I used to get women like that.

He catches his reflection in the shop window. He grimaces at how old and withered he looks, and the flashes of grey that is working its way through his receding hairline.

His eyes focus back onto the shop assistant who is staring back at him a little perplexed, he smiles at her and waves.

Did I really just wave? Yeah, I thought I did. She must have thought I was a right weirdo.

He continues to walk down the street and slots his hands into his jacket pockets.

Oh, course she thinks you're a weirdo, you just spent the last five minutes visually molesting her. Plus, it was a window full of women's shoes you were looking at.

He starts to laugh at himself.

Excuse me, miss, but do you have a red stiletto in a size 11?

He laughs again. This time out loud and again comes the eyes of the bewildered pedestrian, brow contorted, nose wrinkled all in wonder of what weird John is laughing about.

Could do with some of that action though. She was hot and I'm horny. Horny and still need a shit, not a great combination.

Then the cramps hit again, rapidly stabbing into his gut like flaming hot needles.

Jesus!

He doubles over in pain as the IBS express comes powering into the station.

Okay, I'm going to have to really go now.

Clutching his stomach and clenching his anus as tightly as he can he waddles like a penguin down the high street.

Well, if people didn't think you were weird before they do now.

He notices the public toilets up ahead and quickens his pace.

He breaks wind, his eyes growing wide like a deer frozen in headlights.

Oh, crap that was wet. I hope... I pray I didn't follow through, or else I'll have to get rid of these undies.

John makes a sharp turn into the public toilets, not the most glamorous of places but when it's time to go, it's time to go. The toilets themselves are old, in much need of a makeover and modernisation.

John stands at the top of the concrete staircase that leads straight down into the dingy toilets.

John's nose immediately recoils as if it was trying to climb up his face and his nostrils flare from the putrid smell of stale urine that has wafted up to greet him.

"Bloody Hell! That reeks!"

He thinks twice about actually going down the staircase but then his stomach groans again and echoes down the stairs, John knows he will have to follow it. He does.

Grasping the rail tightly he cautiously makes his way down the chipped and cracked steps. He is not cautious due to fear of falling you understand, but the fear of filling his pants before he reaches his goal.

He reaches the foot of the stairs and into the uninviting dingy public toilets. It's empty. It is not just the smell of urine now (which is even worse than it was while he stood at the top of the stairs), it is now unpleasantly mixed with a pungent aroma of human faeces and a hint of vomit.

John gags and almost vomits himself, feeling it bubbling up his throat like a boiling kettle. But he manages to suppress it and returns to darkest depths of his bowel.

The dingy room is lit only by two buzzing tubular bulbs, that flash on and off as if they were two swordsmen caught in a flashing duel.

To his left, fitted into the greasy duck egg tinted wall tiles are a row of four mirrors, well maybe not quite four, the remains of a broken mirror clings to the wall by rusted screws in each corner of its square frame. The other mirrors consumed in graffiti, mostly by the word 'DICK SPLAT" untidily marked horizontally across them all in thick black spray paint. The small sinks hang like a row of grumpy gargoyles who have seen better days.

He surveys the situation and notices that four cubicles stand before him.

He approaches cubicle number one and pushes the door open, which shrieks like the hinges in a haunted house, he immediately recoils taking a step back.

"Fuck!" he whines, again fighting against his own gag reflex and somehow winning again. The bowl filled to the brim with faeces, of all shapes and shades blending together in an overflowing lagoon of human waste, the colour of English oak.

Cubicle number two has no door. John asks himself whatever happened to the door? And why would anyone steal a toilet door? These things remain a mystery.

The bowl itself wasn't too bad, in need of a good clean, the remains of past consumers visible through smears of excrement that streaks the porcelain.

John thought about using this toilet for a second but didn't fancy doing his business and someone walking in and gawking at him during such a private moment.

Cubicle number three, was again filled with large clumps of human waste bobbing up and down in the golden brine like floating buoys. Unfortunately, no seat.

He pushed the door open to cubicle number four to be met by the stench of vomit. Again, John takes a second to get over the initial shock of the stench burning is nasal passages and he clamps his nose with his thumb and index finger.

"Christ almighty"

Then looking inside realises there is no toilet, just a hole in the floor where it once sat. Vomit replacing water that would have once consumed the pipe.

"Number 3 it is then I guess" he says in an almost quack, still gripping his nose.

He walks into cubicle 3 and closes the door behind him. No bolt.

"Fucking typical" he groans.

He leans over the toilet and yanks the rusty chain that hangs from the old cistern, fixed to the dirty tiled wall above the toilet.

It gurgles and churns, the floaters and water in the bowl starts to rise, John takes a step back fearing that it will over flow, but just as it looks like the contents will cascade from the bowl, it suddenly retreats and is flushed away out of sight leaving clear(ish) water in the bowl.

John sighs with relief.

Turning his attentions to the toilet itself, seat less and the rim tacky with the remains of dried on stale urine.

"Don't fancy touching that" he grimaces and looks around, "yes!" He says in surprise a roll of toilet paper half full is wedged behind the long slender pipe that rises up to join the cistern. He starts to unravel a big handful of toilet paper and then gives the rim a good wipe, staining the paper with a sickly looking orange. He grimaces and drops it into the toilet, the water immediately consuming it and it starts to dissolve.

Still not taking any chances he begins to place pieces of toilet paper around the rim, it starts to resemble a Christmas wreath collage, but halfway around pain strikes again.

"Oh shit, oh shit, oh shit."

Quickly John unbuckles his belt and whips down his trousers

and pants in one rapid movement before dropping down onto the cold porcelain below.

There is the charming sound of his internal contents leaving his backside and splattering the bowel below. The relief is almost euphoric. He leans forward to hold the door closed with his hand and continues his onslaught on the toilet bowl, unloading the contents of his gut like an AK47.

"Oh, that's better." He says in utter relief.

As he sits there on the cold tacky porcelain, pieces of toilet roll starting to stick to his buttocks.

As his backside continues to orchestrate a cacophony of random flatulence, his eyes start to wander and he explores his surroundings. The two slim board sides and door were home to hundreds of marker scribbles and drawings in a riot of colours, working its way across the spectrum with the majority in thick black. His arm grows tired, so he gently removes it from its job of holding the door closed, the door gently opens a little bit, but not enough for any arrivals to see King John on his throne.

His eyes start to focus in on the unintellectual scribble that devours the tedious grey cubicle.

God is alive and well.

Dicky Jones.

FUCK YOU.

Bitchface.

Did I dream that?

A fart is the lonesome cry of an imprisoned turd.

"Fucking Hell!" John chuckled

I'm sorry it was all a mistake.

It's his Mom in the end.

We are the dreamers of dreams.

RIP George Michael.

Working Class Hero is something to be, I guess.

The Chamber of Secrets has been opened.

A.D.I.D.A.S After Dinner I Did A Shit

Close your legs, your brain's catching cold.

John was captivated now by the walls of gibberish, but was it all gibberish? Some actually made sense to John and he found himself nodding along in agreement with the scribe.

Like... Do you Idealise the past? Or see it as broken? Why?

May your life be like a roll of toilet paper, long and useful.

Who the hell is Gordon Bennett?

Change your life, not the channel.

His eyes roam right until he spots two screw holes that would have once homed the toilet roll holder. Above it, it says Pull here for art degree.

John giggles again and shakes his head and continues to read the right side of the wall.

Anyone can piss on the floor. Be a hero, shit on the ceiling.

Roses are tits, Violets are tits, I love tits, tits, tits, tits.

God is love. But Satan does that thing you love with his tongue.

Eat less ham. Do more push ups.

Cockneck.

Red Alert

3-P

Don't drink and drive, take acid and teleport

Things I hate. 1. Lists 2. Vandalism 3. Irony

Knock, Knock.

My Butt-cheeks have graced this surface, as have yours. And for that, we are brothers.

WWJD

Mom is that you?

That tape is unnecessary.

Stay close to the toilet, it's not as big as you think.

Clive was here '88

Donkey Dick

"Donkey Dick! Jesus!" roared John "I haven't heard that since I was at school."

Scrotum Pole

Kick him in the nards!

Why can't you people poop at home

Free smack for all guests

I'm watching you...WOW your dick is small.

Michael sucks cock. And I'm amazing at it. Take a bow Michael.

Fire at will! Why? What's he done?

Why is it so hard to get fucked?

John allows his mind to wander away from the tales being told by the cubicle walls and focuses on what he has got to do the rest of the day.

I'll pop in to see mom later, she only lives around the corner, don't see her as often as I'd like, especially since dad left her. Still haven't figured out why he left, arsehole. I always thought they got on.

His gaze comes across the hole that has been cut into the cubicle wall. Arrows drawn by marker pens point to it and the word 'Old Glory' is scribed across it.

John starts to think of the girl in the shoes store and how sexy she was. He imagined her taking off her blouse. Unbuttoning it slowly to reveal two pale, pert breasts. She takes down her auburn hair and swings it from side to side like something out of a shampoo ad. His penis rises from the shadowy toilet bowl and stands to attention between his thighs looking up at him.

"Oh fucking hell, now I have the horn."

He gazes again at the hole and notices a phone number written underneath it and the words 'You know what to do'.

He takes out his phone and writes out a text, before pressing send he thinks about just having a tank and being done with it, but his dick looks up at him almost begging him. It had been such a long time since it had been handled by a female that he thought rigor mortis had set in.

"What the hell!"

He sends the text message.

Immediately he gets a reply. The sound of his beeping cell phone echoing through the empty room.

The text message reads 'Two minutes, I only live around the corner. Wait for me.'

"Oh, wow. This is going to be amazing!"

Then his mind wanders and fixates on a drawing of a clown laughing.

Wait?! Maybe it's not a woman! Oh shit! What if it's a man. Oh shit, what am I going to do? Of course, it's going to be a man,

John you idiot! This is the men's toilet!

He thinks about leaving and attempts to stand up. That's when he hears the sound of high heels coming down the stairs and into the toilet, coming closer and closer.

Phew! It is a woman. Thank God! Could be a transvestite.

Oh shit. Oh shit.

The footsteps carry on to the next cubicle and stop. He shallows hard.

"Put it in the hole." Comes the whispering murmur of a female.

He relaxes and breathes a sigh of relief.

At least it's a woman.

He stands and slots his dick into the hole. It disappears to the other side and then he feels the gentle grip of a hand grasp it.

Whoever is on the other end of the cubicle works it like a seasoned pro and John has to lean on the cubicle wall to hold himself up. He is in ecstasy. He can hear her tongue lapping up against his pulsating manhood and he so wants to cum She knows, and she vigorously tugs on his shaft.

You can't cum yet, it hasn't been long enough. Why not? You haven't got to buy her dinner or cuddle with her afterwards. This is perfect!

He ejaculates. And there is silence for the longest time. He hears the toilet flush next to him.

Was she having a shit too?

"How much is that?" He asks.

"Twenty dollars." Comes the voice from the other side.

His eyes grow wide and he has a sickening feeling swirling in his gut.

"Mom?" He asks.

"John?" Comes the reply.

A groan of disgust fills the room as The Elvis laughs.

"I think we have a winner." Announced The Host.

The Elvis stands up and takes a bow.

"I'm here all evening!" he laughs.

"You better hope that wasn't a true story!" The Marilyn says smacking him playfully in the arm. "I have a story." Says The Jesus.

"One that can top that?" The Host asks.

"Yep!" The Jesus nods.

"Well, then let's hear is JC." adds The Groucho.

He stands and takes strong stance as if he is reading Shakespeare on a stage. He clears his throat.

"In the beginning God created the heavens and the earth…"

He is interrupted by a mass bombardment of half-eaten bread rolls and a serenading of boos.

Chapter 4

Franklin

The afternoon sun reflects violently on the large glass windows of Wellington's Drug Store. What once was a small family run business of just one tiny shop in Barnville's High Street that was founded by Cecil Wellington and his wife Phyllis, the store was left to their only child, Thomas. He went on to expand the company into the several neighbouring towns and cities, such as Studd City, Forge City, Sanctuary as well as into Canada in Blackfoot Ridge, a few years ago before selling it to a conglomerate which has now taken it nationwide with a Wellington's in every major city in the United States. But, gone is the quaint single windowed shop that once stood instead replaced by the monstrous pop up stores that are now commonplace.

The sound of Franklin's keys that hang from his belt loop can be heard jangling through the aisles before he is ever seen. Along with the tapping of his smart shoes skipping off the hard tiled floor and the awkward squeaking of their taught leather, together it is an unusual melody of sounds, a cacophony that has become commonplace in this particular branch of Wellington's, his trademark if you will.

The middle aged Franklin pushes his glasses back up his nose as he saunters down the herbal remedies aisle, before disappearing through two double doors that lead to a back stockroom area. The doors flap back and forth before gently settling back into place. Suddenly the doors swing open again with the force of a trolley bursting through them causing them to go through the same process again. The trolley is stacked with various boxes and bottles of stock, and Franklin pushes it while a whistle and a squeaky front wheel joins his orchestra. His small puny frame struggles but just about manages to get the hefty trolley rolling and up aisle 3 and turning sharply to the left towards aisle 6 but then turning again into aisle 5 and settling there, pulling with all his might to stop the heavy trolley that was really rolling with momentum behind it.

He straightens his uniform, trying to straighten out any wrinkles and creases to his pale grey trousers and his mint green short sleeved shirt. He adjusts his name badge and glasses again before focussing on his trolley and stock he must find homes for.

He rips open a box and takes out some long slender bottles of turquoise mouthwash. He places them onto the shelf, one that is clustered with various brands of mouthwash in a rainbow of colours. He stops for a moment and looks around at the overly white building, everything in its interior is sickly white.

He sighs.

There must be more to life than this.

He pushes the trolley further down the aisle and fills up the gaps in the toothpaste.

I've been here for twelve fucking years! I know every price of every item in this shit hole! I know where everything is, and I know everything that's going on.

Franklin continues to stock the shelves like some android programmed to do one thing and does it over and over again, repetitively, without having to think about it. A flickering strip light gets his attention and for the moment he pauses to look up at the light that hangs from the buildings high ceiling.

I wish my life was as exciting as that light. Seems to have so much going on even if it's dying out and needs to be replaced. I have nothing in my life that could warrant that kind of seat of the pants excitement. Look at it, flickering away like it's bouncing around the dance floor of some rave, even though it knows it will probably be replaced by Reg the maintenance man tomorrow. Yeah, that's what is called living in the moment. I wish I had the balls to do that. Or even something worth living life to the full for.

He goes back to what he's doing. Finishes the stocking of the aisle and moves on to the next one.

He comes to a halt halfway down aisle 8. Plasters and Dressing. He starts to fill the gaps and then notices he has a clear view of the registers. An attractive red-haired teenager sits at the till, playing with her hair and gnawing on a chunk of bubblegum, her demeanour portraying that she is bored and uninterested. Franklin stares at her.

Yes, I said I know everything that goes on in here.

A smartly dressed bearded man walks across his view and he winks at the girl who returns a flirtatious smile.

I know that Jill on till 3 is screwing the boss.

Franklin remembers just last Wednesday, while working the late shift, The Manager said that Franklin could leave early and that he and Jill would finish up.

Heck, what could I say, he's the boss. And who wouldn't want to get home early?

The Manager and Jill stare at Franklin, fake cheesy grins etched on their faces waiting for him to leave so they can get up to no good. The Manager locks the door behind Franklin and as he leaves they both wave at him insincerely, teeth gripped together probably saying 'Thank God he's gone'.

Yeah, he's a lot older than her and has a wife and two kids at home. She's just turned 19. The dirty fucking bastard! They think that nobody knows. But I know. I know because I watch them.

Franklin stands outside in the cold and the pitch black of night and watches as they aggressively kiss each other as he paws at her blouse, ripping it out from the tight waistband of her skirt, awkwardly undoing buttons, fingers and thumbs as she quickly undoes his belt buckle like seasoned professional. A sharp yank to his zipped fly and his trousers and underpants are down, dropping like a broken elevator, ground floor. He still fumbles at her buttons but as she grasps his growing penis in her grip, he doesn't even bother to try an unbutton the blouse any longer, instead he rips it open and buttons fall around till 3 and bounce on the hard-tiled floor. He pulls her bra up so her pert breasts fall out underneath and he sinks his face into her cleavage, then licks and suckles at her firm nipples.

Yes, I watch I always watch. I guess it's a little sad, maybe even a little sick. But like I say I have nothing else in my life.

The manager lifts Jill's tiny frame up with ease still kissing each other passionately and he plants her firmly on the small conveyer-belt of till 3. Her skirt riding up to her hips exposing her slender stocking covered legs, that wrap around him and pull him in as if she is a human lasso, yearning for him to be inside her. He pulls her heart printed panties to one side and eagerly penetrates her with all exuberance and finesse of a jackhammer.

I always watch, come rain or shine I stay and watch. Sometimes I jerk off. Does that make me a bad person? A sick person? I have nothing. If anything, this is my sex life. I'm involved in a ménage à trois, only they don't know I'm involved.

With each vigorous thrust of the manager's pelvis the electronic till beeps comically and with that something pulls him back to present day, a slight erection levering its way up between his legs, pushing on the crotch of his trousers.

"Excuse me, young man!" comes a voice which immediately snaps Franklin out of the daydream altogether.

"Oh!" he says startled "I'm sorry I was miles away!" and looks to an elderly lady standing next to him smiling a denatured smile. He returns the smile and realising he has an erection still protruding, he manoeuvres himself behind the trolley.

"How can I help?" His face contorting into a counterfeit smile of unease.

"Could you tell me where the haemorrhoid cream is?"
In his head he sighs.
This is my life.

"Certainly Madam! Aisle 2, third shelf down."

"Thank you, young man!" and with that she shuffles away down the aisle.
It's a sad state of affairs when the nearest I will ever get to anal sex is by showing some old broad where the pile cream is.
He sighs again, this time out loud, his will to live seems to leave with the long-lasting exhale.

I'm a forty-four-year-old Jewish virgin. I still live with my mother who is completely deaf and going senile. I live on a diet of homemade brisket every night and I work here six days a week. And to make matters worse I'll never get laid because I resemble Adolf Fucking Hitler. Man, I'm depressed! I sometimes wish I was dead.

Franklin takes out a pack of razor blades. He stares at the packet. Frank tears open the razor blades and holds a razor blade in his fingertips, the light gleaming from the sharp blade. Suddenly he jabs the blade into the main artery of his left wrist. A Vesuvius of blood erupts from his wrist and sprays his face. He starts to stagger down the aisle, the blood spraying into the air and showering passing customers who scream at the sight of seeing the blood spraying out of his wrist like a garden sprinkler. It covers the old lady with the haemorrhoid cream, it covers Jill's

80

gobsmacked face, her gum falling from her widening gape, it sprays over his manager who is shouting his name at him.

"Phone call for Franklin Schmerling. Phone call for Franklin Schmerling!" comes the crackle of the tannoy speaker. Franklin snaps from yet another vivid wool gathering moment and places the razors back into the box, before making his way to the manager's office, accompanied by his accustomed soundtrack.

CHAPTER 5

LEONARD

A succession of quaint little shops huddles together on the corner of Vigo and Tully in Forge City's market district. One of them sticks out from the rest, a comic book store called Ka-Boom! The bright orange and white signage bursts out from a jagged explosive surround, like the sound effects on a comic book page. The sign helps the shop to jump out from between the bland gift shop, bakery and thrift store fronts. The row of shops all sit adjacent to the best flea market in the city.

A large obese man leans on the counter engrossed in a comic book, his elbows set either side of the comic, his fat chin resting on bulbous hands, rowed with chubby sausage like fingers. Totally engrossed in words of enchanted escapism. Ignoring the three customers that shuffle around the store, exploring comics themselves or looking at figures or collectibles of their favourite comic book characters.

The fat man scratches at his scruffy beard that patches his blubbery cheeks and then scratches and tugs at his under wear that has ridden up the crease of his bulbous backside. So lost in the comic and the constant scratching he doesn't notice a flash of fur scurry across the shop floor in front of him and hide behind a stand stacked with this weeks new releases. The fat man crams one of his stubs into his nostril and rummages around as if digging for gold with a sausage shaped pick. The flash of fur passes by again, unbeknownst to the fat man.

Suddenly, a man wearing a large furry Wookie mask from the Star Wars franchise jumps out in front of the fat man growling loudly like some furious grizzly bear, flailing his arms around in the air. The fat man shrieks a high pitch shrill, a sound you would never have thought could come out of such a beast of a man, so loud, so feminine.

Muffled laughter can be heard from inside the mask as the fat man holds his chest, his breathing pattern changing rapidly.

"Goddamn it, Lenny!" he pants "You fucking asshole! One of these days you're going to give me a fucking heart attack! D'you know that?"

"I live in hope!" Lenny says removing the mask, revealing a large cheesy grin and wild dark hair in disarray, as if he'd stuck his fingers in an electric socket.

Lenny jumps up onto the counter, unveiling a set of knobbly knees protruding out of a pair of khaki cargo shorts, some odd socks and a pair of dirty baseball sneakers, laces untied and dangling down towards the worn old carpet that lies beneath.

"So what ya doing, Lou?" He asks snatching the comic from the counter and flicking through the pages much to the annoyance of Lou.

"Reading! What's it looks like?"

"It looked like you were picking your ass and sharing it with your nose from where I was standing!"

"Give me that!" Lou snatches the comic out of Lenny's hands "Haven't you got anything to do?"

"Only to annoy you chubby!" he says hugging Lou's sweaty bloated head and squeezes it tightly planting a big kiss on his head.

"Will you get off me!" Lou groans "I hate it when you're in this mood"

"But I'm always in this mood?"

"I know!" Lou says staring at him through squinted eyes, before the pair burst out laughing.

"So, what's the plan of action for today?" Lenny asks playfully swinging his legs back and forth.

"Well, I thought I would just sit here, on my fat ass, for the next eight hours and read comics."

"That sounds like a fucking plan to me, boss!" Lenny shouts jumping up to his feet standing on the counter and addresses the customers at the top of his voice like some crazy town Cryer. "Ladies, Gentlemen, Klingons and Middle Earth virgins! I have an announcement to make!" The few customers in the shop turn to face him, all regulars so they have all seen this type of thing from Lenny before, many times.

"Today's plan of action is this!" he mimics unrolling an imaginary scroll and holding it out in front of him as if to announce something very important.

"We! (That's me and Lou or Lou and I) We will be doing Fuck all!" and with that rolls back up his invisible scroll. "Thank you for your time!" he adds bowing before the customers, who roll their eyes and go back to what they were doing.

The phone rings, gyrating across the counter top with each ring, Lou picks up the receiver "Hello Ka-Boom, you've got Lou!"

Lenny puts the Wookie mask back on his head and jumps down off the counter and starts to growl again loudly.

"Yeah, sure I'll just get him." Lou holds the receiver out towards Lenny who is now stomping around like Sasquatch.

"It's for you, Chewie!" says Lou handing him the phone.

"Hello?" He answers, his voice muffled by the mask "Yes, it is a bad line!" and with that takes off the mask and throws it at Lou. "Is that better? Great! Oh, Hi Anna! Yeah sure I'm free! Really?" he whistles enthusiastically nodding his head and motioning to Lou by rubbing his thumb and index finger together, showing that he is coming into some money "Okay, thanks. Bye, bye!"

"I'm gonna be in the money, chubs!" he shouts.

Chapter 15

The Elephant in the Room

The empty soup bowls are taken away by the waiter as the guests clean up by dabbing at their lips with their napkins. The conversation dies and there is a moment of silence.

"Could you get us some more wine please?" The Host asks the waiter.

"Certainly, sir!" he says with a nod of his head, his hands filled with soup bowls which he places as gently as possible down into a serving trolley, which when full, he pushes out of the room and the rattling of the ceramics and cutlery stowed on top can be heard as it rolls out into the hallway and towards the kitchen. Again, there is an awkward silence.

The Host remains silent, but with a smile on his face. Most hosts would see their dinner party as a complete disaster if the conversation was as dead and as silent as a cemetery, but he continues to smile, a smile of satisfaction. The guests look around at the room, at their host, at each other, fleetingly making eye contact all of them thinking of something to say and wondering why The Host isn't making the effort to save his soirée.

It could be that he is taking this time to appreciate who sits in front of him and be proud of what he has actually accomplished here (granted they're not the real personas that they parade as, but in his eyes, he has accomplished a massive feat). The skipping of the waiter's shoes can be heard ricocheting on the hard- tiled floor once more as he returns with more wine.

"Ah! Here's the wine!" The Host boasts "You'll all have more wine, yes?" he asks smiling a toothy grin, that kind of strange smile that a person gives you that knows something you don't, a grin that teeters on the verge of being sinister.

The guests smile and nod and hold out their empty glasses for the waiter to fill them, he makes his way round the table and fills their glasses again.

"Excellent!" The Host says clapping his hands together.

"Thanks Sugar." The Marilyn says to the waiter with a flirtatious wink and she takes a sip, her lipstick printing itself onto the rim once again.

The waiter leaves, closing the doors behind him.

The Marilyn focuses on the empty place that is set and with a little reluctance asks, "Can I be the one who asks about the elephant in the room?"

All the attention turns to The Marilyn now, probably all thinking the same thing.

"What elephant, my dear?" The Host asks through gritted teeth, he knows what elephant she speaks off and he's starting to get annoyed with The Marilyn.

87

Trust it to be her who brings it up! The fucking bitch! Ruining things! The others wouldn't have said anything about it!

"The mystery of the missing guest?" she answers.

His eyes burn into her pretty pale face and sensing the awkwardness in the air, The Groucho attempts to dilute it with a joke.

"One morning I shot an elephant in my pyjamas. How he got in my pyjamas I'll never know!"

The Host swiftly adjusts his gaze to The Groucho and frowns "I'm sure you've already made that quip?"

"Well," The Groucho says looking a little nervous by The Host's peculiar glare, but thinks on his feet, "Regurgitation always repeats itself."

The Host's demeanour changes again and he laughs long and loud at this.

"I know, I know it's a shame that the evening I had initially planned hasn't turned out quite as I had hoped." He leans back in his chair and takes a glass of water from the table, preferring it over the wine this time and gently sips at it.

"The guest was unavoidably detained, and unfortunately it came too late in the day to find a suitable replacement."

"Wer was es?" (Who was it?) The Adolf enquires.

"Oh good, a guessing game!" The Host bursts out "This will occupy us until the main course arrives! Would anyone like to have a stab at it?"

They all look deep in thought, frowns rippling across their foreheads, squinting eyes, the internal cogs turning at such a rate now. Not that it would matter if anyone got it right or wrong, but like any gathering of human beings, that competitive instinct kicks in and everyone wants to win.

The Jesus being young and naive doesn't give himself long enough to think about the question and he blurts out "Mickey Mouse!"

He is met by several confused stares.

"Dummkopf!" (Idiot!) Says The Adolf shaking his head.

"What?" Asks the blushing Jesus.

"He's a cartoon character!" The Elvis sniggers.

"Oh!" The Jesus meekly answers, the scarlet blush of embarrassment consumes his face and he sips his wine, deciding to sit this one out.

"Yeah, Sugar! The guest has to be a real person."
The Marilyn says flashing a sympathetic smile his way.

"He is real! My sister has a photograph with him!" The Jesus spurts out and is immediately met with wide eyes and sniggers.

"She has one with Pluto too!" he adds but looks around and just stops talking and sinks down into his seat. Hoping that it will consume him and his embarrassment.

"Please stay in character!" The Host snaps "Jesus Christ didn't have a sister and she didn't visit fucking Disneyland!"
The table bursts into laughter and even The Host joins in, and just like that the conversation is flowing again.

"The next time I see you, remind me not to talk to you."
The Grouch quips at The Jesus who crosses his arms and sulks.

"Do you know something I think Jesus did actually have a sister. I'm sure I've read something about it." The Elvis adds.

89

"That maybe so!" Says The Host "But there's no way she went to Disneyland."

A wave of laughter rounds the table again, The Jesus, sulking at becoming the butt of the joke.

"So, who do you think it is?" The Host asks bringing down the laughter and the thinking faces appear in front of him once more.

"Winston Churchill?" Says The Adolf.

"No." answers The Host.

"Abraham Lincoln?" says The Marilyn.

"You do have a fascination with presidents don't you, Marilyn?" Chuckled The Host shaking his head.

"David Bowie?" Says The Elvis.

"Good one, but no." answered The Host.

"Mahatma Ghandi?" Guesses The Groucho with a shrug.

"No." answers The Host.

"You can Pat my Ghandi anytime!" The Grouch says wiggling his cigar between his fingers that had become a trademark of Groucho Marx.

"So, who was it?" enquires The Elvis.

The Host smiles and says "Well, it was..."

CHAPTER 6

JODIE

At intervals of about every 10 seconds, the dark bedroom was lit by a glowing red neon light, splicing through the open slatted blind, it bathed the one room apartment in a glow of pink horizontal flashing stripes.

The grunting and groaning of sexual pleasure fill the room and is subdued and overpowered on occasions by the shrieking of SCPD's finest and their wailing sirens.

The curvaceous silhouette of a female grinding vigorously can be seen on the damp back wall of the room in neon stripes before darkness and then returns in time with the glow of the strip club signs from outside.

She rides her customer (A Mister Piper) like a jockey grips a saddle, her thighs straddling either side of his motionless middle-aged overweight body. She arches her back, running her hands though her short dark hair, sending it into disarray and causing it to stick up in various directions. She pants, heavily and then squeals, her breasts flailing in every direction, beads of sweat flicking from her nipples.

She gyrates faster and faster, flicking her pelvis forward, the constant rubbing of her pubis' makes her pant even more and squeal again with pleasure. Mr Piper's body remains as rigid as a corpse, his hands no longer groping for her ample bosom like they were at the beginning of this escapade, but now down at his sides, fists clenched with intensity. His face mimics his hands as it scrunches up into an ugly grimace, sweat filling the craters of his face now, as his teeth grind tightly on each other. He'd never be able to have a woman like this, not without paying for it anyway. She grinds faster and faster now as she is ready to reach her climax. He has been ready for the past five minutes and he's just trying to hold on. Thinking of anything to make him last longer, an ugly politician, replays of last night's Angels game, even the image of his grandma pops in there at one point, it all helps because she is destroying him with every expertly placed thrust.

Suddenly she switches gears as if the racehorse is on the home stretch and can see the finish line in sight. Faster and faster she thrusts now, the bed springs constantly squeaking now and the headboard thumps against the already cracked plaster. Mr Piper grips two handfuls of the sodden bed sheet in his hands and holds on, he knows his time riding the roller coaster is coming to an end. She groans, and he ejaculates. He erupts with an almost deafening growl of euphoria ending with a loud "FUCK!"

She sighs with annoyance and a sharp roll of her eyes, yet again she didn't get to finish, but ever the professional she collapses next to him and tells him how amazing he was and that nobody has ever made her come like that before. Heck he's a man and probably won't know the difference whether she faked it or not.

"Oh, Jodie!" Mr Piper pants wiping his sweaty bald head with the back of his hand "That was amazing... you are amazing!"

She waits for it. The sentence that always follows.

"You're so much better than my wife."

"Thanks!" she says climbing off the bed and heading for a dresser that homes several wigs, her cell phone, a bottle of water, a packet of Freebird's cigarettes topped with a disposable lighter and a packet of half used baby wipes.

Jodie aggressively rips a couple of sheets from the packet before throwing them onto the bed next to Mr Piper, who has already got his socks on. Jodie wipes her vagina with a look of boredom and normality on her face. She lights a cigarette and takes the time to inhale deeply, as again she is bathed in the neon glow. As she turns around still naked with only a cigarette to keep her warm, Mr Piper is dressed and ready to leave.

"You really are extraordinary Jodie!" he says sifting through dollar bills in his wallet "I'd ask you to run away with me, but I know what the answer would be." He adds smiling at her, holding out a considerable amount of hundred-dollar bills.

She takes the money and smiles "But Mr Piper, you're a married man!"

"Yeah..." A wave of depression smothers him, "Yeah, I am."

She opens the door and lets him out.

93

"Same time next week?" she asks.

"I'll damn sure try!"

The door closes, and she locks it and then fits the security chain into place.

"Fucking hell! What a jerk!" she says falling backwards onto the bed, cigarette still clasped between her plump lips.

"The lightweight couldn't even wait for me to finish!" she takes another drag on her cigarette, blowing out the smoke and watching it change colour as the neon continues to flicker outside her window. She flicks it into the ashtray that sits on the bare wooden floorboards next to the rickety old metal frame of the bed.

"I guess I'll have to finish myself off, again!" she says slipping her fingers between her legs and caressing her drenched labia and then rubbing at her clitoris. Her cell phone rings and completely destroys the moment.

"For fucks sake!" she growls.

Chapter 7

Henry

Henry sits on an old worn deckchair on the fire escape of his high-rise apartment, a mug of coffee gripped in his wrinkly hand. He smiles to himself as he takes in the warmth of the morning sunshine on his dark skin. Traffic whistles past underneath him as the city goes about its business, but this doesn't affect old Henry who has lived here in Studd City all his life and has grown accustomed to the sounds of the city, so much so that he hardly notices it. He zones out and swigs his coffee while looking out above the protruding buildings that reach heavenwards for just a peek at the cloudless sky, which is painted in a glorious cobalt shade as if an artist had just transferred it from pallet to canvas in one swift stroke.

"Hot diggidy damn! What a beautiful day!" Sighs Henry with a cheeky school boy grin on his round and wrinkled face.

"What a day to be alive, yes sir! What a beautiful day!" He says again lifting his old bones up from his old foldout chair. The cartilage in his weary old knees scream but he doesn't seem to notice, not today, not on such a beautiful day like this. Besides he's used to any ailment his body can throw at him now. Arthritis, gallstones even the cancer, he's battled that demon before and won.

He stretches out his back and leans on the railing of his fire escape and watches the people running around below, off to work, shopping, or their daily routines.

Henry has become quite the people watcher, better than television he tells anyone that will listen. He knows everyone's routines now, well the regulars anyway.

An old black man shuffles along the sidewalk below him with the help of a cane like some awkward tripod from War of the Worlds.

"Ha! Right on time!" he smiles.

"Good morning, Burt!" he calls down and is met by a wonderful contagious smile.

"Hi, Henry!" he calls back accompanied by a wave which Henry mirrors.

"You're getting slower old man!" Henry jests.

Burt laughs and slaps his thigh in response, "Shrapnel!" he laughs "No trumpet today?" Burt calls.

"No, Sir! She's inside." Henry indicates with a pointing thumb over his shoulder towards his open window of his apartment "Goddamn neighbours have complained again!" he grimaces shaking his head.

"But you play beautifully Henry! Always cheers me up when I'm passing by." Burt smiles.

Henry holds his arms out, spilling a little of his coffee down on the grated fire escape.

"Eh, what can you do!"

"Have a good day, Henry!" Burt waves again before leaving.

"You too, Burt!"

Henry slowly climbs back through his window and back into his apartment, the air conditioner below the window coughs and splutters like a patient in a clinic waiting room.

"I best get some practice in if I've got that gig tomorrow night." He says grabbing his old trumpet that stands on top of his old television set. A moment of confusion sweeps across his face "Or was it tonight? Damn, I think she said it was tonight!"

Chapter 16

The Main Course

A succulent piece of steak sits in front of each guest. The recipe, Italian stuffed steak, three sirloin tri-tip thinly sliced steaks filled with bread stuffing and shaped into rolls as it lies on a bed of spaghetti sauce. The sauce is also drizzled over the steaks and then sprinkled with mozzarella cheese. The guest's mouths water and several moist tongues can be seen flicking in and out to lick their lips, like a vivarium full of lizards awaiting their meals.

"For those of you that are of the Jewish persuasion, I would like to inform you that your steak is kosher!" The Host pleasantly announces.

Steam rises from the meal as the guests tuck in with heatedly enthusiasm. The Host cuts through the steak with his knife and fork and watches as the slightly underdone meat exudes some blood.

The Host smiles as he lifts the fork with the piece of steak on it, momentarily looking at it, as beads of its juices drip from it and onto the plate.

"Rare! Just how I like it!" he says plunging the fork into his mouth and chews the meat, slowly. He closes his eyes as he savours the flavour.

Perfect. Everything is going perfectly. What a truly magnificent Dinner Party! One of my best yet, if I can be so bold! If I was to make my opinion on these characters from tonight's proceedings... Jesus is a wet lettuce (note to self, if I book Jesus again, be sure to get an older one) Adolf is an astute individual and his German is flawless. Groucho is my favourite, I think. Elvis is hot, and I'd fuck him. Marilyn is hot, and I'd fuck her, may have to gag her first though, she does have an annoying way of interrupting. Louis has hit the mark splendidly. But the evening is not over yet, but I must remember that this collection cannot be revised. It's a once in a lifetime gathering. No matter how I feel I shall not duplicate a Dinner Party.

He places his knife and fork back down onto the plate when he finishes chewing on his first forkful.

He pans around the table observing his guests, who are enjoying their meal immensely.

"Are you all enjoying your meals?" he asks.

They nod relentlessly, their mouths full, chewing like cattle.

"I am glad. The chef is exceptional. Italian of course! I believe Italians are always the best chefs." The Host adds as he vigorously cuts another piece from his main course.

"Don't you agree, Elvis?" he asks, trying to build up the next topic of observation, which is obviously food.

The Elvis looks up with a mouthful, bulging in his cheek, like some squirrel storing his nuts.

The Jesus looks up at The Elvis, confused and with a mouthful of food he talks, spraying a little food into the air.

"Why are you asking him?"

The Host turns to Jesus, looking baffled and a little disgusted at Jesus' outburst.

"Do you care to enlighten us to your outburst, Jesus?" The Host adds annoyed but intrigued.

"He's not Italian!"

"So?"

"Well, you're singing the praises of Italian chefs, he's not even Italian. Anyone can cook!" The Jesus nonchalantly shrugs.

The Host bubbles and simmers, letting himself cool off.

Don't ruin this. It's going too well. Fucking idiot kid! Breathe.

"It's called a conversation! And yes, Italians are the best chefs, no argument! Besides, this particular chef happens to be a culinary genius because it was yours truly!" he smiles ready to soak up the adulation of the guests, who do not let him down and all tell him how wonderful it is.

"Well, anyway, the guy lived on fast food and died on the crapper..." The Jesus intervenes spraying more pieces of his meal everywhere "...Stuffing his face with a greasy hamburger! So, how would he know anything about a chef's culinary skills?"

Elvis puts down his knife and fork. His forehead contorts into an exasperated scowl and angrily growls

"Hey, Jesus! Fuck you!"

The Jesus' eyes grow wide in disbelief and nearly chokes on his latest mouthful as The Elvis rises from his chair. Everyone watches with nervous anticipation, no longer focused on the delicious food, but on The Elvis, who looks ready to explode.

The Marilyn rises with him and softly squeezes his arm, "C'mon, let's calm down."

The Elvis looks at her and nods before returning to his seat.

"I know good shit when I eat it, and this is good shit! Probably the best steak I've ever had!" The Elvis states "My hat is off to our host on this one."

"Oh, it was nothing really!" blushes The Host "I prepared it earlier on today. The meat was ever so fresh! In fact, all this evenings delights have been prepared by yours truly."

"De meinst, du hast keine Küche voller Leute, die da hinten herumgeschlichen sind?" (You mean you don't have a kitchen full of staff slaving away back there?) The Adolf asks in awe.

"No, I only hire a waiter for these little gatherings. I cook and prepare everything myself. He only has to dish it up and serve the courses. Oh and of course the wine. Which he is probably drinking now!" Says The Host chuckling a little which is then mimicked by the rest of the table.

The Elvis then points his fork at The Jesus "For your information, The King did not die on the throne."

"No, he died on a cross. I'd have been cross too if I was him!" quips The Groucho who is shut down by a glance of The

Elvis' eyes. "I'll see myself out!" Says The Groucho hands up indicating he won't get involved in such a personal subject.

"He was found on the bathroom floor."

"Okay, okay. I'm sorry!" apologises The Jesus.

They all go back to eating their meals and silence falls on the dinner party, only the sound of cutlery on china plates can be heard.

"So, what's your favourite food Sugar?" The Marilyn asks The Elvis who spurts out "Hamburgers." without a hint of irony. The table explodes with laughter leaving a dumbfounded Elvis in its wake, he then realises and joins in too.

"Oh, how ironic!" The Jesus quips "Whose burgers d'you like?"

"Whose?" The Elvis answers confused.

"Yeah, you know; Mindy's, Bernie's Smokehouse, Franken's?" The Jesus adds.

"Oh, Right! I'd have to say none of the above. I like to make my own!"

Everyone looks at Elvis, now intrigued at the possibility of him having any culinary prowess. It is simpler for them to see each other as the people they portray and not the real person underneath, obviously because they have been forbidden to get to know that persona underneath the wigs and flamboyant wardrobe. They probably see The Elvis dancing around his kitchen in a brimstone studded jumpsuit and blue suede shoes.

The Host doesn't know one way or another, whether Elvis was a good cook, so he lets this one play out. Plus, he is what's known as connoisseur of food and he is always intrigued by the possibility of a new recipe to add to his own repertoire. As he cooks with lots of different kinds of meats, this could be something he could definitely utilise.

"Please, do go on Elvis. You have my undivided attention. I have a lot of meat in the deep freeze and I'm yearning to try out some new ideas." Grins The Host.

"Es ist schwer, Rindfleisch Burger genau richtig zu bekommen." (It's hard to get beef burgers just right.) The Adolf says talking as though he might know a little about cooking too.

"It sure is!" The Elvis chortles, nodding in agreement "It's taken me years to perfect it."

"How do you make them Sugar?" The Marilyn asks, a twinkle in her eye now as she stares at him, seeing more than just a handsome face now.

Good looking guy, speaks German and now he can cook? This guy's got more layers than a fucking onion. I might have to get his number after this charade is over.

"Well," The Elvis starts to explain but, in his head, he is in his trailer park home and standing behind his kitchen work service. The trailer is piled high with Elvis Presley memorabilia, from records, posters, statutes and dozens of other pieces.

"First of all, you'll need about one pound of minced beef." He says slamming it down onto the chopping board and kneading it a little, probably to the sound of The King on stereo, possibly 'I Just Can't Help Believin' which happened to be his particular favourite.

"One medium sized onion, one egg and six sun-dried tomatoes!" Which happen to all be lined up in front of him on his work surface.

"A teaspoon of cumin seeds and 1/4 of a teaspoon of cayenne pepper. Remember, a 1/4 of the cayenne pepper, you don't want to blow your fucking head off with it. You will also need four white bread rolls, sliced cheese..."

"Welche Art von Käse?" (What type of cheese?)
Interrupts The Adolf.

"I don't think it really matters. Whatever kind you like. Where was I?" The Elvis asks, no longer able to visualise what he's doing.

"You were talking cheese." The Marilyn says, returning him to his kitchen where he continues to talk about what ingredients will be needed.

"Yeah, so cheese! You'll need about four slices. Mustard or tomato ketchup, whatever's your preference, and four small lettuce leaves. Oh, and a pinch of salt and pepper."
The Elvis takes a sharp kitchen knife and starts to chop the onion, rapidly like a true professional.

"For prep, you want to peel and finely chop the onion."
The Elvis' knife slides the chopped onions into a pile, knocking the excess off by violently hitting the blade on the chopping board, the rest of the onion drops off and joins the rest of the finely diced pile. He then takes the sun-dried tomatoes and starts to chop them too.

"Also, you want to chop up the sun-dried tomatoes." Elvis picks up the pound of minced up meat again and slams it into a glass bowl.

"Then you want to knead and mix the minced beef in a bowl." His rough thick hands squeeze and squash the meat between his fingertips he works it around he bowl.

"You've gotta use your hands, it's the best way to kneed it just right."

The Elvis picks up the chopped onions "Then add the onions and mix it up again." He slides them into the bowl, before scooping up the pile of chopped sun-dried tomatoes.

"Now, my secret is to add sun-dried tomatoes."

"In die mischung?" (Into the mixture?) The Adolf asks again.

"Yes, Sir!" answers The Elvis with a nod of his head.

"Wait a minute!" Asks The Marilyn with a bemused look in her face. "What the hell is a 'Mischung'?"

"Well, whatever's missing, I didn't take it!" quips The Groucho.

"The Mixture!" comes the response by The Host, The Elvis and The Adolf simultaneously blurt out, in such unison it was if it had been practised.

"Oh right, carry on!" she says yawning a little. The Host sees the yawn out of the corner of his eye and seethes again, not a lot, just a little but enough for him to snap at her.

"Is Elvis boring you, my dear?"

"Oh! No! Not at all! I just feel a little lethargic tonight that's all. Please do continue." You can sense the truth in her defence, she likes The Elvis and the last thing she wants to do is to offend him. She's just genuinely tired.

You try grinding three dicks in one night and see how awake you are! Asshole!

"So, yeah, sun-dried tomatoes!" The Elvis continues, his sticky hands kneading all of it in together.

"Then add the rest of the ingredients. The egg; crack that bad boy in there! Now, you wanna really get that mixture kneaded."

The Elvis then sprinkles the cumin seed and cayenne pepper into the mixture.

"Then just a sprinkle of the ground cumin seed and cayenne pepper and you're ready to shape those little mothers!"

The Elvis then shapes the mixture into four patties, bulging with pieces of onion and tomatoes.

"Then throw those little buggers under the grill."

"How long do you grill them for?" asks The Host.

"I say around seven to eight minutes. About four minutes on each side." The Elvis answers "Then you're ready to rock n' roll!" he smiles, in his muse he slides a steaming hot patty that spits and sizzles on its journey down towards the waiting bun, that is topped with a fresh lettuce leaf.

"Slap on that slice of cheese and top it off with and hefty dollop of ketchup!" he says squeezing the second bun firmly on top.

"That's how you make the perfect burger." He beams.

The table erupts with applause, so The Elvis stands up and takes a bow.

CHAPTER 8

TO THE LUSCIOUS VELVETY TONE OF DORIS DAY

Jodie slides a tape into her old boombox that has served her well since college, snapping the door shut on 'Jodie's Mixed Tape' she plunges the play button down until it clicks and reels start to turn. There is a moment of crackling and then the luscious velvety tone of Doris Day bursts out of the speakers, with her rendition of the song 'I enjoy being a girl'.

Jodie stands in her apartment again illuminated by the constant neon flicker, as she stands wearing nothing but her matching set of ivory coloured underwear. She dances over to her bed and picks up the infamous Marilyn Monroe white halter neck dress that lay on the bed that just thirty minutes ago was covered in a plastic sheet that was sodden with Jodie's own urine. This particular customer is a urophile and enjoys taking part in the fetish known as water-sports.

Franklin approaches his old mahogany wardrobe that stands in the corner of his bland but incredibly tidy bedroom at his mother's house. His scrawny body clad in white loose-fitting boxer shorts that appear to have been ironed, and black dress socks, which are pulled halfway up his shins. He slides out an immaculate khaki Nazi uniform jacket.

Floyd soaks in an old stained bathtub, his long sodden hair covers his face with the only thing protruding from his face is a dwindling joint. The smoke floats upwards past the shower curtain that is riddled with patches of damp and then circulates the dripping shower head. The droplets falling every twenty seconds and splashing in the murky greyish bathwater, that looks like something you'd empty out of the kitchen sink of a busy restaurant.

Hanging on a hook of the bathroom door is a long linen robe, swaying slightly in the draft entering from under the door, it sways in the hot moist steam like some ghostly apparition.

Bobby looks at his reflection in the long full-length mirror, topless in his tight black leather trousers and pointed toe, black, smart leather shoes that have a slight heel. His bare torso is illuminated by a single lightbulb that hangs from the ceiling, the muscular definition of his tanned body is made more prominent by the light, much to the delight of Bobby who flexes like some bodybuilder, before breaking into some pelvis thrusting like the king himself.

Lenny's room is dimly lit by a lamp on a bedside table made from house bricks. A bed can be seen with an exposed mattress, sheets and quilt left in disarray on top of it. Clothes are scattered all over the floor, maybe it's the maid's day off?

An old bulky television set sits on a broken cupboard. On the screen, through a flickering snowstorm of a picture, is the movie

'Some Like It Hot' - the scene in which Tony Curtis and Jack Lemmon are first seen in their disguises as Josephine and Daphne, as they arrive at the train station. The walls of the room are covered with posters of vintage movies, Casablanca, The Rat Pack's Oceans 11 and Citizen Kane amongst various others.

Lenny stands in his tight underpants looking at himself in the mirror, but no physique that would be at home in a bodybuilding competition here. He scrunches his face up like a gurner and glances around the room before looking at his reflection pointing at his protruding ribcage asking the question "Are you talking to me?"

The torrential rain lashes down on the elderly Henry's window with reckless abandonment seemingly without a thought or a care that Henry will have to step out into it in a short while. He wets his lips, slowly rubbing his tongue over his bulbous bottom lip. He then wraps them around the mouthpiece of his Henri Selmer B-Flat trumpet, as if it were the lips of a beautiful woman but instead of making love, he made music.

Jodie's eyes are locked in a deathly stare as she flicks at her thick eyelashes with thick black mascara. They flutter like wings of a hummingbird in search of nectar, the beauty of such a sight is matched only by the two blue pools that shy away under the lashes.

Lenny brushes black grease paint above his top lip, laying it on thick and bold. Slotting the cigar into the corner of his mouth he practises "...You wouldn't be here if it wasn't" shaking the cigar and shuffling his already greased eyebrows in time with the cigar like some strange conductor.

Franklin purses his lips together tightly, a fish face staring back at him like a blowfish. He presses a toothbrush style moustache into place above his upper lip.

Bobby runs the teeth of comb through his greasy jet-black hair, its slickness shining in the light. With hair grease in his hands he drives them into his long hanging fringe and manipulates into the desired shape of the classic pompadour style.

Floyd sits on the edge of his bed, towel wrapped around his waist and his dripping hair concealed by a second towel. A cloud of smoke surrounds him as he enjoys his marijuana joint. Blowing smoke rings high into the air, like native American smoke signals, signals saying that Floyd is in no hurry to get ready.

Henry expertly fingers the buttons that rise and fall from the valve stems with ease as he warms up his arthritic fingers for the evening ahead.

Jodie pouts her full lips together as she swabs bright red lipstick over them, their plumpness resembling a freshly picked juicy ripe strawberry. She playfully blows kisses at herself in the mirror, getting into character she presses an artificial mole into place on her left cheek and licks her shimmering lips.

"Happy Birthday, Mr President!" She smirks.

Franklin holds in his hands a symbol that struck fear into the hearts of millions of people for many years, a symbol that's origins are much different from how they are perceived today due to one man's prejudiced views and abuse of power. This symbol in Hinduism means prosperity and luck but that was changed to mean antisemitism and terror. He sighs and then pulls up the red Nazi arm band over his khaki officers' jacket and securing it into place around his upper left arm.

Bobby slips on his black leather jacket, that matches his pants and zips it up halfway concealing his tanned muscular torso underneath it.

Floyd sits on the toilet straining aggressively as he tries to force out his two-day overdue stool. The joint still prised between his lips as his face is scrunched up like a ball of unneeded scrap paper.

Jodie's hair is fitted neatly into a stocking as she applies a blonde wig, which is set in a windblown and soft waved fashion. A hairstyle that has become synonymous with Marilyn Monroe and looked upon today as iconic.

Henry applies the mute to the action end of his trumpet and blasts out a rough version of 'Someday', before stopping and smiling. With the smile he mimicked his lookalike perfectly.

"He once said, 'I warm up at home. I hit the stage. I'm ready, whether it's rehearsal or anything!'" He laughs a gravelly laugh that seems to be stuck in his throat "And I'm exactly the same."

They all stand steadfast in their differing surrounds, in front of mirrors to take in their transformations.

Jodie bends over forwards provocatively squeezing her breasts together creating a bulging and inviting cleavage, clad in her famous white dress, kissing and winking at the mirror.

"If I'd observed all the rules I'd never have got anywhere."

111

Bobby grabs a handful of his fringe and with a flick of his wrist whips it into the King's style and gyrates his hips and with a little shimmy, he raises the corner of his top lip.

"Don't be cruel."

Henry straightens up his smart blue tuxedo and slots his trumpet into its custom-made carry case and secures the latches to lock it. Still the rain attacks his window pane with malice.

"Damn! Looks like I'm gonna need the umbrella tonight! I'm gonna be more like Gene Kelly out there!"

Franklin viciously clicks his heels together standing to attention and raising his right arm straight into the air for the infamous Nazi salute.

"Sieg Heil!" (Hail victory!) He yells before sticking his middle finger up at his reflection saying,

"Hitler, Sie Hahn Sucker!" (Hitler, you cock sucker!).

Lenny skulks around twiddling his cigar between his fingers reciting some famous quotations.

"I have nothing but respect for you -- and not much of that." He cackles before striding away from the mirror.

Jodie's tape comes to an end and it shuts off. The satisfying sweetness of Doris Day ends, and the play button flicks itself back up to join the others ready to be used again.

A flushing sound erupts from the bathroom of Floyd's apartment and he shuffles out wearing nothing but a pair of stained underpants that look as though they have never seen the inside of washing machine drum. His brown leather sandals on his feet and robe clenched in his fist. Hobbling out he looks a little out of it, resembling a zombie rather than someone that is about to portray the son of God for a Dinner Party.

"I suppose I should get ready for dinner." He manages to groan before swaying to and fro for a moment and then ultimately collapsing, unconscious, onto his unmade bed.

Chapter 17

Not Everyone's a Christian

The clanking of cutlery echoes around the room as knives and forks are placed down on empty plates. It sounded like a sword duel in some old black and white swashbuckling movie, most likely starring Errol Flynn or Douglas Fairbanks.

The Host wipes his mouth clean with his napkin that had sat comfortably in his lap. The plate in front of him is empty, leaving behind just a small puddle of blood from the steak, mixing with its natural juices and the course's seasonings making it appear amber in colour.

"Well, that was delicious!"

The guests are all surprised by yawns, all feeling a little tired after such a large portion.

The waiter returns to the room, his timing impeccable, it wouldn't be proper to leave the guests staring at their finished plates. He swiftly takes the plates, stacking them expertly on his arm, something that is made quite clear he had down thousands of times before.

"We'll have another bottle if you please!" The Host says looking up at the waiter, smiling. The waiter leans forward and mutes his voice to a whisper "I'm sorry Sir, but we don't appear to have any more bottles." Almost embarrassed.

"No need to worry young man. There are plenty more bottles in the wine cellar."

"Oh, okay Sir, then I will retrieve another bottle!"

"Open as many as you like!"

The Waiter leaves, juggling the plates on his arm but not struggling too much to close the doors behind him again.

"Here's a question for you!" The Host asks sipping his water, "With all the illustrious famous figures we have sitting around this table, who do you think is the most famous?"

The table stirs with a collective rumbling of excitement of such a question.

"That's easy!" The Marilyn scoffs with a dismissing attitude.

"Go on, Marilyn?" The Host answers intrigued already.

"Jesus! It has to be Jesus." She answers finishing the last dregs of her wine glass, tipping her head back as far as it would go as if to get every last drop.

"Yes!" The Jesus rises holding his arms out either side of him and nodding to everyone.

"Why thank you Marilyn!" Then grasping his half empty wine glass, he holds it aloft into the air. "Now, gaze upon me as I turn thy water into wine!" His over-elaborate manner causes everyone to laugh and he takes a sip "Oh! It's already wine! Then my work here is done." And with a nod of his head he sits back down to more laughter.

"Blessed are the cracked, for they shall let in the light." The Groucho says quite poetically.

"But JC isn't necessarily the most famous." The Host adds, much to the astonishment of the table.

"Blasphemy!" The Groucho squeals in an over the top comical reaction.

"Woruber edest du? Naturlich ist es Jesus!" (What are you talking about? Of course it's Jesus!)

"All I am saying is, not everyone's a Christian." The Host adds holding his hands up in the air as if to warn off their disagreeable gazes.

"What's that got to do with it?" Asks The bewildered Elvis.

"Exactly what I said. Not everyone on this planet believes in Jesus. I don't, I'm an Atheist." Shrugs The Host.

"Ich glaube nicht an den Weihnachtsmann, aber ich habe immer noch von ihm gehort." (I don't believe in Santa Claus, but I have still heard of him.) adds The Adolf.

"Whether you believe in him or not, you still know who he is (or was). So, therefore, I stand by my statement and say that Jesus Christ is the most famous person ever!" nods The Marilyn as if to put an end to the conversation.

"Maybe, Adolf was closer." The Host adds, met by yet more confused faces.

"Was meinen Sie?" (What do you mean?)

"Santa Claus! I think he could be the most famous person ever." The Host states "Everybody knows who he is."

"Yeah, maybe!" The Elvis nods "But, the question was, 'Who do you think is the most famous around this table?'"

"So, we all agree, I am the most famous?" The Jesus grins, looking very arrogant, like no depiction of Jesus Christ ever.

"I believe I have a valid shot." The Elvis says leaning back and holding his arms out wide, welcoming a debate. The guests look at him in disbelief. The Host picks up his glass of water and takes another sip before leaning back into his chair and smiling, excited to see where this particular conversation will go.

"Du sagst also, dass Elvis bekannter ist als der Sohn Gottes?" (You're saying that Elvis is more well-known than the Son of God?)

"Why not?" The Elvis says folding his arms in defence now.

"Sorry Sugar, but I've got to side with the Nazi on this one!" The Marilyn says patting him on the shoulder in pity.

"Why the hell not? Elvis was... I mean, I am a singer and a movie star. When you are in the entertainment business you can reach a lot of people." He boasts, getting very defensive about it all now and a part of him wishes he hadn't said the statement in the first place, but pride has intervened now. It's nudged him over to the passenger seat and it's driving the ego mobile now.

117

"I'm free of all prejudices when it comes to Elvis movies, I hate them all equally!" Smirks The Groucho in terror.

"Screw you clown!" Seethes The Elvis.

The Groucho holds his hands up and mockingly shakes, "Quote me as saying I was mis-quoted."

"The King has left his mark on Hollywood." The Elvis counts on his fingers as he states each movie with passion, "Jailhouse Rock, G.I Blues, Blue Hawaii, The Trouble with Girls; all great movies!"

"Indeed!" Agrees The Host "Did you know Elvis starred in 31 movies from 1956-1969?"

"You see!" Beams The Elvis with all the adulation of a proud parent "31 mother fucking movies, people! Beat that Jesus!"

"Well then, the same argument could be made for Marilyn!" Jesus states.

"What, you mean flops?" The Marilyn coyly laughs.

"No way!" shrieks The Groucho, breaking character for the first time that evening, "I mean...Erm..." Unable to think of a witty response blushes as red as a cranberry.

The Host joins his blush but with a little hint of anger that pumps blood into the vein on his neck for a split second and then is controlled.

"What Groucho is trying to say, and making a complete mess of it, is that your films were very good! And that Marilyn Monroe had a very successful film career. Arguably more successful than Elvis!"

"Really?" asks The Marilyn with a bemused and unconvinced look on her face.

"Das ist wahr! Marilyn war in einigen tollen Filmen!" (It's true! Marilyn was in some great movies!) The Adolf agrees.

"Did you know that Marilyn starred in 33 movies from 1947-1962?" The Host adds another well researched statement to help the conversation along.

"Ooh! 33!" The Marilyn perks up "Beat ya, sugar!" playfully sticking out her tongue at The Elvis, who can't help but smile back at her.

"This guy's like a living, breathing movie encyclopaedia!" The Elvis scoffs shaking his head in disbelief at The Host's knowledge of film.

"Gentlemen Prefer Blondes was always my favourite." says The Jesus.

"How to Marry A Millionaire!" Adds The Groucho.

"Seven Year Itch!" nods The Adolf.

"All great movies! I think they might have you there, Mr Presley." The Host says, stirring the pot.

"Come on guys! They're only chick flicks!" The Elvis announces to anybody and everybody.

"The same as yours! Only girls went to see them. That's why they did so well, not because you could act."

"Ouch!" The Elvis replies and can't help but laugh at The Jesus' burn.

"Manche mögen's heiß" The Adolf announces slamming the palms of his hands down onto the table, making the cutlery shake. His reaction like he has the answer to the sixty-four-thousand-dollar question.

The Host excitedly nods his head in agreement with The Adolf "He is right!"

"Yeah he does have a point there. I bow down to you there Marilyn!" adds The Elvis as he lifts his arms up in conceded defeat.

Marilyn looks on, confused and frustrated, obviously not being able to speak German she is totally lost.

"Hello?" She calls sarcastically "Will somebody tell me what he said?"

"Adolf made a very good argument about why you may well be even more famous and made an exceptional movie that trumps anything The King ever did."

"And what movie was that?"

"Manche Mögen's heiβ!" The Host reiterates, then adds "Some Like It Hot!"

A buzz of excitement flows through the room.

"Ah! How did we forget that one!" The Jesus groans.

"Surely the greatest comedy ever?" The Elvis announces "It's most definitely up there!"

"Such a beautiful movie!" adds The Host nodding with agreement.

The Marilyn with little knowledge of film looks unconvinced and she takes this time to light up another cigarette.

"So, you're telling me..." she says blowing fresh cigarette smoke out of the corner of her lips "...That because of that one movie I'm more famous than Elvis and Jesus?"

"Hey, I've been in a few movies too, you know!" Scoffs The Jesus, playfully.

"Ich auch!" (Me too!) adds The Adolf

"Religious preaching and war propaganda? Well, I'm free of all prejudices. I hate everyone equally!" Scoffs The Groucho.

"Now, Groucho here, he's been a star of movies for over 40 years! You can't go that long in the film industry without having a following or are well known." The Host announces, to which The Grouch raises to his feet and takes a bow.

"Why, look at me! I've worked my way up from nothing to state of extreme poverty!"

"Haven't we gotten a little off topic here?" The Marilyn says through another cloud of smoke.

"Have we?" The Host looks at her through a squinted face of puzzlement.

"Well, yeah. I thought that this discussion was about who was the most famous. This has become a 'my dick is bigger than your dick' debate." She answers, "And there's no way I can compete with that is there?"

"Of course!" laughs The Host "I do apologise."

"Look, at the end of the day, it doesn't matter what you do; it's whether you reach the people and connect with them. That's what matters." Elvis states.

"Very true." The Host agrees again with The Elvis (not for the first time tonight).

Oh, we connect. He's everything I dreamed The King would be. He's been an obsession of mine since... forever. I wouldn't say I

121

was a homosexual. I like women, Hell! I'm married! But I can find a man attractive. Guess that would make me bisexual by today's standards, if you want label it. But, yeah, I would fuck this man. He makes my loins smoulder.

"So, how would you even calculate a thing like who is the world's most famous person ever?" The Elvis asks, bursting The Host's perverse bubble.

"A vote?" The Jesus says putting forward a solution.

"Sicher, in der heutigen Zeit ware das Internet der Schlussel dazu?" (Surely, in this day and age, the internet would be the key to this?) The Adolf states.

The Host smiles and sips his water.

"Funny you should say that, because I have the answer and it does involve the internet." He smirks, everyone looks at The Host with bated breath. There is a moment of silence and anticipation, like a roomful of actors waiting for the envelope to be opened and the recipient of the Oscar to be revealed.

"So, you know who it is?" The Elvis breaks the silence.

"Yes." The Host answers smugly.

"You mean you've known all this time?" asks The Jesus "Man, you could have saved us some time!"

"But then we wouldn't have had such a thrilling discussion!" The Host grins again.

"So how did you work it out?" Asks the intrigued Marilyn, leaning her elbows on the table, her breasts squeezed together tightly unveiling an impressive cleavage for all to see.

"And more importantly who won?" Jesus laughs.

"Two words." The Host grinned "Social media."

"Twitter?" says a confused and surprised Elvis.

"Well, for this particular experiment I used Facebook." The Host boasts, loving having all the facts and having them eating out of the palm of his hand. They are so involved now that they want to know. They need to know. They must know.

"Over 2 billion people use Facebook every single day and a lot of them create 'Fan Pages' so that people can continue to support and show their affection for famous people long after they're gone." The Host adds.

"Sie sagen also, es gibt eine Fan-Seite fur Adolf Hitler?" (So, you are saying there is a fan page for Adolf Hitler?) The Adolf shakes his head in disbelief that anyone would make or even follow a page devoted to remembering Mein Fuhrer.

"Well, no not really!" The Host says chuckling to himself, "There are a number of parodies that make fun of Hitler, but unfortunately for you, you're out of the competition."

"Oh!" The Adolf moans, wrapped up so much in the character that he is actually disappointed that he will not be the most famous individual sitting at the table.

"Now the important factor is who has the most followers on the said pages?" says The Host delving into the inside pocket of his tuxedo revealing a golden envelope.

Everyone looks on with disbelief and anticipation.

Marilyn shakes her head "This is the craziest dinner party I've ever been to!" and takes another drag on her cigarette, giving off a trail of smoke that snakes around her as debris of ash falls like snow to the white cotton tablecloth below.

The Host stands to his feet and adjusts his jacket before opening the envelope and pulls out a white card.

"And the winner is..."

Chapter 10

Say, Aren't You...

The lonely dark street in a part of town you wouldn't want to wait around for long, Jodie stands wrapped in an unflattering trench coat as she waits under the circle of white light that shines from a long slender streetlight.

She could be mistaken for a prostitute, which isn't too far from the truth, but selling it on the streets? No, that's not her style, she's above that. She will continue to make her money in the comfort of her own home, either through phone call bookings or emails. Sometimes she can make just as much from her live sex shows that seem to be all the rage at the moment.

Her coat and dress cascades against her as the wind blows along the street. Luckily, she doesn't have to wait around for long. A Ford Lincoln Town style taxicab in classic canary yellow and sliced through the middle with a scar of black and white checkerboard, slowly rolls up to the sidewalk and the off/on duty sign light on the roof of the cab goes off, indicating it has a customer. She opens the door and slides into the back of the taxicab, slamming the door behind her and shuffles her backside on the seat until she finally gets comfortable on the hard-black leather.

"Cecil Avenue, please." She asks making eye contact with the driver's black wrinkled face in the rear-view mirror. His bald head nods "Sure thing, Miss!" he replies.

For a couple of minutes, they sit in silence with just the roars of the concrete jungle outside. Jodie drifts off and glances at the mismatch of buildings that lean on each other like a row of drunken sailors propped up against a bar.

He glances at her several times his eyebrows contorting each time, the look you give someone you meet that you think you know or have met before. His constant looks start to make her feel uncomfortable, to the point where she is contemplating telling him to pullover, but then he speaks.

"Say aren't you..." He starts but is immediately interrupted by Jodie, now realising that she is dolled up like Marilyn Monroe and that is why he is staring at her.

"No!" She sighs rolling her eyes "She's fucking dead!"

"But you..."

"That's the idea!" She snaps sarcastically "Just drive!"

"Okay, okay!" he says turning his attentions back to the road. But he continues to glance at her every chance he gets, maybe it's because she looks so much like Marilyn Monroe or maybe he is staring at those long legs that lay crossed exposing her shimmering stockings. Legs that were just three hours ago wrapped around a client's head, muzzling him with her vagina.

126

She rummages in her white leather purse. She takes out a cigarette and presses it between her plump red lips. She flicks the lighter and an amber glowing flame rises, dancing in the darkness of the taxi.

"I'm afraid there's no smoking in my cab, Miss." he states shaking his head to and fro.

She sits with the cigarette hanging from her mouth, with the lighter flame still flickering and cuts the driver a look that could curdle milk. The driver smiles, a gold tooth twinkles as he does so.

"But! Seeing as it's you! I'll make an exception."

She smiles "Thank you!" and ignites the cigarette.

"Damn! Are you sure you're not her? You look just like her!" he says, shaking his head in disbelief still not able to take in the inevitable truth that she isn't the real Marilyn Monroe.

Marilyn rolls her eyes again and shakes her head as she takes the cigarette out of her mouth and exhales, the slate coloured smoke rises and twirls around the rear of the taxicab looking for a way to escape.

"Are you going to a fancy-dress party?"

"Something like that!"

The taxi driver now notices her legs and adjusts the mirror to look at them, her dress riding up with the motion of the journey. He licks his lips as the top of her stocking exposes itself, flashing the buckles of her suspenders as it rubs on her muscular thigh.

"You're even more beautiful in person!" the driver murmurs.

127

"Hey!" she yells, catching him in the act, she adjusts herself and the startled driver's eyes return to the road once more.

"Keep your eyes on the fucking road and do your fucking job!" she growls

"Sorry, Miss!"

"Pervert!"

A long uncomfortable silence rears its ugly head and the tension could be cut with a knife. Again, the driver tries to make small talk, seemingly never to learn his lesson.

"How about that rain last night?" the driver says cutting the silence with his croaky grizzled voice. She nods but doesn't reply.

"I'm just glad it's cleared up now. It's a nightmare to drive around here when the weather is that bad."

"I'm sorry, did I call a cab or a mobile weather forecaster?" she snaps.

"What a grouch!" He groans under his breath.

Marilyn turns from looking out of the window and stares at the driver, through the mirror, with a look of surprise on her face

"Excuse me?" she snarls.

"Nothing!" he answers "So how about an autograph?"

She leans back into the seat and looks out of the window again "I've told you..."

"You're not her! Right, I get it. I hear ya," he says winking at her in the mirror "How about an autograph?"

Seriously, how long has this guy been in this cab? Does he really believe that I am THE Marilyn Monroe? What a fucking

128

moron! She's been dead, like, what? 50, maybe 60 years? What a fucking
douchebag!

"I've had them all in the back of this cab, you know. Tom Cruise, Corey Feldman, Bret Lennox, Crystal Stone and now you!"

Marilyn rubs her forehead with her hand, fed up with his constant bullshit.

"I've told you, I'm not Ma..."

"Yeah, sure, it's fine. Your secret is safe with me."

Marilyn shakes her head again.

"Here we are; Cecil Avenue."

They pull up to the sidewalk in front of an old three storey house. The house is lit up at every window.

"That'll be 12 bucks." She passes him $15

"And you're lucky you're getting that tip!"

She exits the cab and the driver quickly winds down the window and hangs a meaty forearm out of it.

"Still no autograph?"

"Fuck off!" she growls slamming the door, before walking towards the house. A gust of wind cuts across her path and causes her dress and coat to rise, reenacting her famous scene from The Seven Year Itch.

"How about a Polaroid?" He calls after her, still unable to let this go.

She turns around and flashes her middle finger at him with all the venom of a pit viper.

The taxi driver shakes his head.

"Man, that Madonna's a real bitch!" he says as the cab rolls away.

Chapter 19

Dessert

As the evening's events move into its twilight, the desserts arrive. The waiter enters through the double doors pushing a hostess trolley. On it is a large silver salver and lid combination that sits in the middle of the trolley, around it is several plates with the evening's desserts.

The Host claps his hands and then rubs them together at the sight of the exquisite slices of strawberry cheesecake, that are all topped with succulent fresh strawberries and a side scoop of vanilla ice cream.

"Ah! Dessert has arrived!"

The guests yawn, and all look a little weary after such an eventful and exhausting evening. The waiter places desserts in front of each guest.

"Dessert is always my favourite course of any dinner party. I have such a sweet tooth." The Host grins excitedly.

"Does anyone else feel weird?" The Elvis says through a gigantic yawn like a pre-hibernating grizzly bear.

"I feel really tired all of a sudden." The Marilyn agrees.
The other guest's nod their heads in agreement all of them rapidly blinking their eyes, looking as though they are all fighting to stay conscious. The Host watches on and doesn't say a word, continually sipping his water.

"I feel so lethargic!" The Jesus says as his limbs fall from the table and hang either side of his body.

"My arms feel like lead!" The Marilyn snivels breaking character and sounding a little alarmed.
The Host's dessert fork slices through the strawberry cheesecake and scoops a piece up, dabbing it into the ice cream, and as it balances, he looks at it salivating before driving it into his maw. His eyes close as he chews and savours the sweet flavours that tantalise his taste buds.

"Ich kann nichts bewegen!" (I can't move anything!) The Adolf groans.
The sound of snoring rumbles through the room as The Groucho is fast asleep, lifelessly leaning back in his chair, with his mouth wide open as drool dribbles down his chin. His moist cigar falls from his mouth, rolling down his chest like a boulder down a mountain face, it bounces before falling into his dessert, the ice cream dousing the burning embers.
The Host continues to eat his cheesecake, oblivious to what is happening to his guests.

"This cheesecake is amazing, I must say. What do you all think?" He asks his waning guests. He looks a little startled as they sit, struggling in their seats, their desserts remaining untouched.

"You haven't touched your cheesecake? Is there something wrong?" he asks, seemingly with complete sincerity.

"We can't fucking move here!" The Elvis cries.

"What's going on?" The Jesus joins in.

"I don't fucking like this!" The Marilyn adds, her scared eyes welling up with a glazing of tears.

The Host returns to eating his cheesecake.

"Oh, that will be the muscle relaxers finally kicking in!" He adds nonchalantly chewing a strawberry as he smiles sadistically through teeth stained a pale pinkish colour.

Chapter 9

What we Play is Life

The Torrential rain beats down in sheets onto Henry's bright yellow umbrella (Well, it belonged to his wife Vivian) but since she passed last July, it's been hung unused on the back of the front door. He thought it looked a little effeminate, but it was raining fire and brimstone out there, so he really couldn't care less. He shuffles towards the front door of an old gothic looking house, that wouldn't look out of place in an episode of The Munsters or The Addams Family. He rings the bell and stands waiting in the rain, trumpet in one hand umbrella grasped in the other.

Henry waits for what seems like five minutes (in reality probably around three, but long enough nonetheless). He rings again. This time pressing the bell in longer so that the shrieking cackle of the chime is drawn out.

Through the glass panel of the front door Henry sees a light.

"Ah! Thank God!" Henry says, for a moment he doubted that he was at the correct house. The Host exits the kitchen, the light from the room behind him illuminating the entrance hallway. He is dressed casually and an apron wrapped around him stained with various food stains.

"Who the hell is this?" He says to himself looking towards the front door. A silhouette of a rotund looking individual with an umbrella stands on the other side. He walks towards the door wiping his hands on a cloth, a look of confusion and intrigue filling his face.

"Who's there?" he calls. His voice drifts away around the high ceiling, circling the beautiful crystal chandelier before working its way up to the first floor.

"It's your favourite jazz horn player, Sir!" comes the reply, the voice croaky, but ever so familiar.
The Host's face glows bright red and the veins in his neck bulge as if they are ready to burst through the skin.

"For fuck's sake!" he growls, wringing the towel in his hands so tightly that his hands appear white and lifeless.

"You're a fucking day early you stupid old bastard! You'll ruin everything!" He purrs under his breath like a seething Tiger.

"Hello?" calls Henry again after another lengthy spell without a reply, "Is everything okay in there?"

"Just a minute!" comes the reply through gritted teeth.
The rain continues to fall bouncing off the dome of Henry's umbrella, cascading down all around him and constantly dripping from each spoke.

"He's ruined everything! I can't do it now! I will have to call the whole thing off. He's ruined it all!" He whispers, the veins pulsate, throbbing with anger "Unless..." He ponders for a moment, and his thoughts (whatever they are) calm him. "Yes, you could do this with five guests, of course you could! You remember the toga party you did, well, Hercules never did show up and you managed to see that one through!" He converses with himself, "Yes I did and that one ended with a bang didn't it?" He nods to himself as he thinks back to the toga party he threw and smiles. He steps quickly towards the door removing his apron as he strides forward, discarding it onto the bulbous newel post that stands proud at the foot of the staircase and throwing the towel towards the door which lands on an antique hat stand that stands behind the front door.

The Host opens the door and greets Henry with a large peculiar smile "Hello Louis and welcome!"

"Good evening sir! For a moment there I thought I was at the wrong place!" he smiles stepping into the hallway and holding the umbrella out the door, shaking off the excess rainwater.

"I was busy preparing things in the kitchen." The Host grins "Here, let me take that umbrella!"

The Host takes the sodden umbrella and hangs it from the hat stand. Water drips onto the hard-wooden flooring, probably damaging it with every drip, "And of course, your coat" The host says, helping him to disrobe and adding that to the ever-increasing number of items that hang from the stand.

"You look great! Really look the part." The Host says.

"Why, thank you sir!" Henry beams and then holds up his musician case "And of course I've brought old faithful!" he laughs that same husky throaty croak that was synonymous with the man he is pretending to be.

"Very good! You'll have to play something for us later on?"

"Of course, Sir!" Henry nods as The Host closes the door behind him.

Henry looks around "Am I the first one here?" he asks.

"Yes, you are a little early." The Host adds "Please, join me in the study for a shot of the good stuff before the others arrive."

"It would be a pleasure!" Henry says and follows The Host into the study, where The Host ushers him to a seat in one of the leather wingback armchairs while he goes to fix them both a drink.

"I always find wetting my whistle with a rich scotch always helps when I've gotta blow that old horn." Henry laughs.

"Indeed!" replies The Host. He hands him a scotch and sits down opposite him.

"Cheers!" He says holding the glass aloft and Henry does the same.

There is silence as they both simultaneously take a sip of their scotch.

"That's mighty fine scotch, Sir!" Henry smiles.

"It is!" The Host replies "Now I have a question for you that may be a little personal, but heck, I'm going to ask it anyway as It's something I have always wanted to know."

"I'm an open book!" Henry laughs "Go for it!"

"But first before I ask, for this evening's events you must stay in character throughout the night." States The Host.

"That's fine and dandy with me, Sir!" he grins.

"Good!" The Host smiles "Now, my question is this. How did you get the nickname 'Satchmo'?"

"Well, when I was just knee high to a grasshopper the other kids started calling me nicknames, I knew everything was all right. I have a pretty big mouth, so they hit on that and began calling me 'Gate mouth' or 'Satchel mouth' and that Satchel mouth has stuck with me all my life, except that now it's been made into 'Satchmo'!"

"Extraordinary!" The Host smiles "Do you just love playing music? I sense that you do."

"Yes, Sir! Music is life itself. What would this world be without good music? No matter what kind it is."

"I'll drink to that, Louis!" And with that, The Host raises his glass again toasting him and swigs the rest of his scotch.
He rises and goes to fix himself another drink "Can I get you another drink?" He asks as he fixes himself another.

"No, thank you sir." says The Louis.

"Would you mind playing me a little number?"

"No, Sir!" The Louis says beaming. You can see the excitement and the joy of playing on his face, he lives for music.

"Is there anything in particular you'd like me to play for you?" he asks removing his trumpet from its case and preparing it ready.

"What do you suggest? Any personal favourites?"

The Host asks sipping his scotch.

"Well, I've always been partial to 'Hello Dolly'!"

"Then go for it my friend!" The Host smiles.

He pursed his lips together and stands preparing the trumpet in front of him ready to play as The Host walks around the room. The Louis fills the room with a beautiful rendition of 'Hello Dolly'. When he finishes, he turns to The Host and smiles.

"Beautiful!" The Host nods grinning intently.

"What we play is life!" The Louis smiles.

"Yes, and what is life without death?" asks The Host, The Louis looks at him confused when The Host launches at him and smashes the scotch glass into his face. The Louis screams and drops the trumpet to the floor. He holds his face that streams with blood, shards of glass protrude from wounds in his face and head.

"You were a day fucking early you moron!" The Host seethes as he retrieves the trumpet and smashes The Louis over the head with it. The poor old defenceless Henry falls to the floor in a heap still holding his head.

The Host then continually slams the trumpet into his head and face as blood stains the horn. Relentlessly The Host hammers him with the trumpet, now bent and broken, until Henry no longer moves, or breathes and the trumpet just sinks into the large hole in the back of his skull. The Host finally runs out of steam and drops the trumpet on his dead carcass before falling back into the chair breathing heavily.

"And I think to myself..." He says through heavy breathes "What a wonderful... world, Hey Louis?"

CHAPTER 20

FAMOUS LAST WORDS

Shock and fear etched on The Marilyn's face, tears start to smudge her mascara creating two black lines that mark her cheeks in uneven lines.

"What the fuck is going on?" she shrieks.

The Host rises to his feet, dabbing any cheesecake debris away from his mouth with his napkin "Oh please don't cry Marilyn!"

"Don't cry? I'm fucking paralysed here! I can't move!" she weeps.

The Host approaches her and whips out the handkerchief from his tuxedo pocket and licks the end of it.

"We can't have you looking like that for your last appearance now can we?" he wipes away the falling mascara tears as best as he can but really only smudges them into her cheeks.

"Last appearance? Goddamn it! What the hell are you talking about!" shouts The Jesus, his face glowing red as he tries to move but can't.

"Tut, tut, Jesus! Blasphemy!" The Host grins walking around the table of paralysed guests.

He stops behind The Groucho who is fast asleep and snoring loudly.

"The Groucho here is a little too relaxed!" he laughs "You see I took the liberty of drugging your wine with a little cocktail of my own."

"Are you fucking crazy?" The Elvis wails.

"Okay, what is the deal here?" The Adolf asks thinking it's all just a sick joke.

The Host sneers at him "In German, please, Adolf!"

"What? No! No more games! Tell us what's going on!" He demands.

The Host marches over to him, that glowing red face rears its ugly head again, but this time there is no need to hold it back. Fuelled by piss and vinegar, he brings his fists down in front of him banging the table, causing The Adolf's plate to jump in the air, the lovely cheesecake toppling over.

"In German!" He screams into his face spraying saliva and pieces of cheesecake all over him.

"No!" The Adolf grows back defiantly.

The Host grabs his face and squeezes it tightly, pulling him in so they are face to face. The Host's eyes glow in his deranged state.

"I said, In fucking German!"

The Adolf looks into his eyes and realises that they are indeed dealing with a madman and that he is in no position to argue, so he cooperates.

"Was ist los?" (What is going on?) He whimpers.

The Host smiles sadistically, patting The Adolf's face before returning to his seat.

Tears continue to cascade down The Marilyn's pale cheeks.

"I don't like this." She snivels "I want to go home!"

"I suppose it's time I told you all what was going on." The Host smiles his demeanour returning to the eccentric party host that started the evening off.

"You bet your ass it is!" spits The Elvis angrily.

"I am..." He stops and ponders for a moment "How shall I put this?" stopping again to think of the best way to put his statement across "I am crazy!"

The Marilyn burst into hysterical laughter, black thick tears still rolling down her face. "Well, that is a fucking understatement!"

"There are many terms used to describe what I am my dear!" He smiles at The Marilyn.

"Insane, psycho, loco, mad, gaga, screwball, brain-sick, demented, mentally confused, disturbed, sick, unbalanced, unhinged, looney, nutcase, weirdo, wacko, cuckoo, mad as a hatter, fruitcake, bonkers, bananas. Well, you get the idea!"

The Host nonchalantly reaches over and grabs The Jesus' plate with the untouched cheesecake and rapidly melting ice cream on it and pulls it in front of him and diving into it with his fork again. He consumes it in just three forkfuls, chewing eagerly and pig like while flashing a smile at his worried guests.

"So, what the fuck is this all about?" asks a worried Jesus "Homosexual date rape party!"

"Well, if your dick comes anywhere near me, I'm biting it off!" snarls The Elvis.

The Host finds this very amusing and bursts into laughter.

"If I was going to fuck you Elvis, it would be in that tight bubble butt you have, not your mouth. I could never damage those silky vocal cords of yours!" He laughs "But, no I'm not going to sexually abuse any of you. I've been there and done that. The great toga party of '99 ended in a right old orgy!"

He finishes the cheesecake and dabs at his mouth again before speaking, "I told you all when you arrived that this was an experiment. An experiment to see what could happen if these famous characters were all sat around a dinner party. What would they talk about? How would they react?"

"So, what is going to happen to us?" The Marilyn sobs.

"Well, first, I am going to finish picking this delicious (and it is delicious by the way) strawberry cheesecake out of my teeth!" a finger drove into his mouth and starts to mine away in between his teeth. He looks around at the scared faces that sit around his dinner table and retrieves his finger from his mouth, wiping his moist fingertip on his napkin, "And now! Well, I'm going to kill you all."

They all remain motionless from the neck down. Beads of sweat forming on their foreheads, trying to struggle but to no avail. But in the back of their minds they still may perceive this as being some game. Until The Host makes an announcement that shows them that it is no game.

143

"Oh!" The Host cries jumping to his feet "I almost forgot!" He saunters over to the hostess trolley "You know when you asked who the missing guest was? Well, he's been here all along!" he lifts up the silver salver with its gigantic domed lid and carries it over to the untouched place that was set at the table for the guest that never arrived. He places it down gently onto the table and lifts the large lid "Here's Satchmo!"

The Marilyn cries.

The Elvis looks away closing his eyes.

The Adolf says something in German.

The Jesus vomits.

The Groucho snores.

There on the silver salver sits the broken head of The Louis. Dents and chunks missing from his skull, his eyes rolled back unveiling yellowy eyeballs, framed with bright red snaking veins. Some shards of glass remain burrowed into his flesh and most sickeningly of all, his trumpet is crammed into his stretched and split mouth, the horn sticking out of him as if he's tried to swallow it.

"I want out of here now!" screams an irate Elvis.

"Oh God! Oh no, please don't do this!" pleads the whimpering Marilyn.

"Settle down. There really is no point in struggling because you won't be able to move!" says The Host standing up again and walking towards the cupboard where the old record player sits. He opens the drawer and retrieves a Korte Combat Revolver .357 Magnum Calibre, which was comfortably lying on the first issue of Playboy magazine from December 1953 with

Marilyn Monroe on the cover. The Host holds up the gun for all to see and pushes the drawer closed.

"I think this has been a very successful evening with great food and great company." He says returning to his seat "You really have been amazing company and made this experience really delightful for me. So, kudos to you all for that!" The Host's face turns from a smiling face to a sad face. He holds the revolver in his right hand.

"But I'm afraid even the most memorable dinner parties must come to an end."

With mascara marked tears staining her face, The Marilyn screams at the top of her lungs.

"You're wasting your time, my dear. No one can hear you." The Hosts says matter-of-factly.

"But the staff? The waiter?" The Jesus pleads terror in his voice.

The Host opens the cylinder and checks the barrels to make sure they are all full.

"There was only one. The waiter, and he had instructions to leave after the dessert was served. And he's already been paid in full, with quite a substantial bonus, too. So, we will not be disturbed."

"What about the neighbours?" Grizzled The Marilyn.

"The Cottingham's? Oh, they are away on vacation in Florida. Until next Tuesday I believe, and the other side is completely empty. But nobody's going to bat an eyelid at a couple of gunshots. Not in Studd City!"

"You're insane!" yells the angry Adolf trying with all his might to move, that he stirs a little. But his limbs refuse to work. The Host pulls the cylinder back into place and, with anger in his eyes, turns to The Adolf.

"How many more fucking times, Adolf! In fucking German!"

The Adolf does not disappoint and screams with everything he has left.

"Du bist wahnsinnig!" (You are insane!)

"I know. I already told you that earlier! Do pay attention." The Host smiles again.

The Groucho wakes from his slumber.

"Ah, Thank you for joining us!" says The Host.

"What did I miss?" The Groucho says in a woozy manner which soon turns into panic "Hey! Why can't I move? And why do you have a gun?"

"Because this crazy fucking bastard..." starts The Elvis but is interrupted by The Host "Be quiet, Elvis. Don't spoil the finale or Groucho. Now remember to stay in character"

"Don't listen to him!" The Elvis snaps.

"We are playing 'Famous Last Words'!" The Host intervenes "What would be your last words if somebody held a gun to your head?"

"Well I..." The Groucho not knowing whether this is a party game or not.

"Don't give him what he wants!" Yells The Jesus, The Marilyn stares at him shaking her head as much as she can possibly move it.

146

"They are helping me to build the scene, Groucho." The Host says gently, trying put him at ease.

"He's lying!" yells The Elvis again "Don't you do it, Groucho!"

"I..." The Groucho stutters confused then his eyes scan the table and see the head of The Louis, the trumpet protruding out of his gullet "Is that Louis Armstrong?" he asks confused.

"Yes, but that was a different party game you missed." Says The Host.

"So that's not a real head?"

"Yes!" yells The Elvis.

"No, no of course not!" says The Host nonchalantly "So famous last words?"

"Well, I've had a perfectly wonderful evening, but this wasn't...."

The Host pulls the trigger and unleashes a bullet with a loud deafening bang. The bullet travels through the air and pierces straight through The Groucho's forehead and exits through the back of his head, spraying blood and bits of brain all over The Adolf. The Groucho leans back in his chair again, but this time he sleeps forever, his body limp and a hole in his forehead. Blood trickles down his face and smoke rises from the hole.

"Oh God! Oh God!" screams The Marilyn.

The table sits open mouthed, frozen in trepidation and fear, their brains not able to take in what their eyes have just witnessed. The Host casually swings the gun around in his hand, its barrel emits smoke like a dragon's snout.

"Now, what are your last words?" he asks no one in particular.

The Adolf struggles flailing his head from side to side as much as he can, covered in The Groucho's blood.

"Get me out of here now!" The Adolf screams, almost gagging.

"For the last time, in Fucking! German!" The Host screams pointing the gun at him.

"Fuck German!" The Adolf erupts and with another blast of the gun, The Host pulls the trigger and a bullet ploughs through The Adolf's face, blood exploding from his wound. His head wobbles back and forth with the impact of the bullet and then his body falls forward, his head falling into the strawberry cheesecake face first. Blood oozes onto the plate, filling it fast until it flows over onto the white cotton table cloth, seeping deep into the fabric and staining it crimson.

"Oh, what a waste of cake." The Host says as the others look dumbfounded as beads of sweat gush from their hair lines wondering who is next.

"Okay, look, can't we talk about this?" The Jesus stammers "You've had your fun, let us go and we won't contact the authorities. I promise you!" he pleads smiling at The Host.

The Host scratches his head with the barrel of the gun. The hot metal burns his head slightly and it makes him pull it away immediately.

"So, if I let you go you won't inform the police?" The Host asks.

"Honestly!" The Jesus beams "You can trust me!"

"I don't know whether I can." Asks The Host.

"You can, you can!" The Jesus pleaded enthusiastically, "Cross my heart!"

The gun goes off again the bullet cuts straight through The Jesus' chest, knocking him off his chair onto the floor. He lies on the floor, dead, unceremoniously his sandalled feet sticking up from his smoking carcass.

"Next!" The Host calls, looking very deranged now.

"Please don't do this!" The Marilyn whimpers.

"What's in it for me if I don't?" The Host playfully toys with her like a kitten with a ball of string.

"I will do anything!" she pleads.

"Shut up Marilyn!" The Elvis intervenes, but he is ignored.

"So what kind of thing could I look forward to Marilyn?" asks The Host as tears gush from her puffy eyes.

"Whatever you want. I will do anything. I don't want to die!" she weeps.

"Shut up for Christ's sake! This is what he wants. He wants Marilyn Monroe's last words!" The Elvis pleads to try to make her see sense.

"I'll suck his dick if it gets me out of this!" she shrieks and then the gun shrieks too. The bullet penetrates through Marilyn's throat; blood flows from it like a raging waterfall as she struggles to breathe and then her eyes roll back in her head and she collapses off the chair to the floor.

149

"So, it's just me and you then Elvis. To be honest with you, that's just how I planned it!" The Host says smiling like a crazed Cheshire cat.

"I'm not giving you what you want." The Elvis growls with defiance.

"Yes, you had to be last. It's been staring you in the face all night too!" The Host cackles but The Elvis remains silent "Oh, you're one cool cat! I guess whoever plays the charade of Elvis Presley must be cool, right? Even up to the end. And you are cool. He must be strong willed. And you are strong willed. And he must be cocky. And you are cocky. If you weren't, then you wouldn't be Elvis and you wouldn't be here. So, I knew you would be sitting here last."

The Elvis remains tight lipped.

"You see there it is hanging on the wall in front of you. Elvis Presley's first feature film, Love Me Tender in 1956. You know what happens at the end?"

He pauses waiting for a response of any kind, but still nothing "I bet you do. Huge Elvis fan like you, I bet you know, don't you?" he pauses again wanting him to fill the gap "No? Why Elvis dies of course. He dies in the end. Quite fitting that you will too." The Host smiles at him and The Elvis returns a sneer, his brain willing his body to move, any kind of movement will do, anything to give him hope, to spur him on. He wills his body to clench his fist. His head plays this over and over again in his head on a loop, trying to trick his body into thinking he has control of it again.

The Host looks on the table to the other end and smiles again.

"So what's it going to be? What would be a fitting last statement for 'The King of Rock 'N' Roll'?"

Elvis just stares at him, scowling at The Host.

The Host stares at Elvis and Elvis stares back; neither of them moving, both locked in a glare.

The Elvis' right arm hangs limp down by the side of his body.

His fingers begin to twitch.

"How about a spot of music?" says The Host springing from his chair, he places the revolver on the table and walks towards the record player and starts to flick through his pile of records.

The Elvis' hand twitches again

The Host continues to flick through the vinyl, all of them Elvis Presley records.

The Elvis' fingers begin to move like the legs on a spider, and slowly he clenches his hand, balling it up into a fist.

The Host stands with his back to Elvis as he continues to look through the pile of records.

"Elvis Presley really made some great songs." Quips The Host.

Beads of sweat gang up on The Elvis' forehead and drips constantly down his face. His arm slowly bends as he lifts it up using all his focus.

The host finds the record he was looking for.

"But here it is. My all-time favourite Elvis song is 'Teddy Bear'!"

The Host turns and smiles at The Elvis as he takes the record out of its sleeve and turns around again, not noticing that The Elvis' hand is on the table and slowly slithering towards the cutlery.

The Host places the record onto the turn table.

The Elvis' hand is inches away from his knife, sweat still pouring from his hair line, through his sharp trimmed sideburns and dripping off his chin.

The record kicks in and the room is filled with that famous voice. The Host starts to sing along to it and dances over the body of The Marilyn as he returns to his seat.

"Come on Elvis, sing along! You know the words!" he mocks with laughter. The Host sinks back into his chair and sways back and forth, clicking his fingers in time to the song and smiling at Elvis. The song comes to an end and with The Host singing along he picks up the revolver in his hand again.

"I just wanna be your Teddy Bear, ooh!"

The Elvis launches the knife, with all the energy he can muster, towards The Host. It soars through the air and impales The Host's upper left side of his chest. The Host's eyes grow wide with shock and he looks down at the knife protruding out of his chest. With the song finished, the sound of the record crackles constantly like the lull of a burning campfire. Blood starts to appear on The Host's white shirt underneath his tuxedo.

"Nice shot!" The Host quips and The Elvis without thinking replies with "Thank you very much!" A grin appears on The Host's face as he aims the gun at The Elvis whose face contorts with the realisation of what he has just said, as the sound of one final bullet explodes from the revolver.

Chapter 18

And the Winner is...

The Host twiddles the card in his hand playfully, almost teasing the guests. He leaves the golden envelope discarded on the table.

"And the winner is..." The Host pauses, a long pause, perhaps too long, but it's all to build up the suspense and prolong the drama. The guests laugh and sit on the edge of their seat, anticipating the results.

"Come on, put us out of our misery!" The Jesus chuckles excitedly.

"The most famous person in this room is..." He pauses again and grins "No, I tell you what we will do; I will tell you in order!"

"The suspense is killing me!" giggles The Marilyn.

"In fifth place with a score of zero is Adolf Hitler!"
Sniggers can be heard from the other guests, but nobody expected anything less.

"Wer hatte es erraten?" (Who would have guessed it?) Laughs The Adolf, before adding "Scheisse!" (Shit!), before playfully sulking in his chair.

"Hey, someone has to be last and it just so happens it was the Jew hating cock sucker that had thousands of people slaughtered and started World War II." The Host adds.

The sniggers turn to laughter and even The Adolf joins in.

"In fourth place... with only 4,158 likes is Groucho Marx!"

The guest boo and jeer hoping that he would have had more.

"Before I speak, I have something important to say!" says The Groucho.

"But in his defence, there is also a Marx Brothers page which has 127,000." Interrupts The Host.

The Groucho gets to his feet, "I'll take that one. And while you're there, call room service and tell them to send me up a larger room." Before sitting back down gnawing on his cigar.

"Now, in third place, with 4.3 million! Is Jesus Christ."

"No way!" says The Jesus "How did Jesus not win?"

The Groucho stands up again holding his finger high up in the air "On Jesus' name I demand a recount!" before sitting down again joined by a plethora of laughter.

"There are a lot of pages related to the concept of Jesus Christ and the Christian belief but I'm afraid as a public figure, it's only third place for you." Says The Host.

"Over one million people is still pretty impressive!" Says The Elvis winking at The Jesus who scowls back at him.

"And in second place!" The Host announces, The Marilyn stubs out her wavering cigarette on an empty side plate and she looks at The Elvis who looks back, they playfully trade scowls at each other.

"With a whopping 12 million!"

The Groucho whistles.

"It's Elvis Presley!"

The guests erupt with applause and The Elvis gracefully shakes The Marilyn's hand.

"I won?" she says

"You sure did. With 13 million!"

"Holy Cow!" she giggles jumping up and spinning around "I'm the winner!"

Everyone laughs and applauds; The Elvis gets up and starts dancing with her.

"The one's famous for her dress blowing up and flashing her underwear, the other for gyrating his pelvis!" moans The Jesus "I walked on water Goddamn it!" and laughs as The Elvis gyrates his hips by The Jesus, his crotch almost hitting him in the face.

"Okay, somebody kill this guy!" jests The Jesus who then pretends to stab at The Elvis with his fork. The Elvis holds the fork to his gut and staggers back to his chair and sits on it pretending to be dead. Everyone laughs.

The Groucho rises and walks over to him and takes his pulse listening to his watch before looking up and says,

"Either this man is dead, or my watch has stopped."

THE END...

...UNTIL THE NEXT DINNER PARTY.

* The Adolf's story translated into English.

JOSEPH

The name's Joseph, but they call me Joey. A lifer, yep safe to say I'm never getting out of here and that's the God's honest truth. I don't know how long I've been cooped up in here to be perfectly honest with you, it's a long time though I can tell you that much.

I could have scraped a tally in here, but they don't like that sort of thing and I don't want to ruffle any feathers, just keep my head down I don't like a fuss these days.

I remember a while back, must be years now but who can tell, I was much younger and stupid, I guess scared is the best word, yeah, I was scared. The first night they put me in here I caused a bit of a flap, oh the hot-headedness of youth. I wasn't going to be told what to do, what I could eat, when I could sleep etcetera no sir, so when they were putting me in this cell I lashed out. Cut one of them up pretty good, drew some blood for sure, but I was thrown to the floor in the melee and my heads never felt the same since. It was all very mentally disturbing anyway and I spent the whole night wide awake thinking that I couldn't live like that for the rest of my days, I had to make the best of this situation.

So, I started to see the positives in things, tried to anyway. I was fed and watered every day, same sort of shit every day but it

158

could be worse, and they kindly gave me the materials that I needed to continue with my sculpting. I feel I can let out a lot of aggression while carving, it's very therapeutic to me. What I create may not look like much to anyone else but to me it is creative expression.

To be honest the cell itself is quite roomy, I mean the last place I was in I was packed in there with six to a cell, I mean you imagine trying to get a bit of privacy amongst that lot, couldn't take a shit without one of their beady eyes staring at me. Caused a lot of fights I can tell you. So, I guess I'm quite fortunate that I have all this space to myself. They did try to put a roommate in with me, which I didn't mind, now what was his name? Pete...no, no I'm wrong it was Percy.

It was long ago, and my mind isn't what it was, but Percy was okay, not much of a conversationalist, but it was okay. Like I said there is enough space to share here. Well, one night Percy was sick, really sick, his head was rocking back and forth vigorously and was throwing up everywhere, the stench was awful. And then Percy just sort of died, curled over and died, lying there in a puddle of his own vomit. I had to spend the whole night with poor Percy, dead.

I tried to make them hear me, but they didn't, and it wasn't until morning that they found him and took his carcass out. The stench of death and sickness lingered for an age.

So yeah things could definitely be worse.

Nothing much else to do apart from looking at myself in the mirror, which isn't fun when you get to my age, you notice every blemish, it gets so depressing. Sometimes I hear the sound of music coming from somewhere, not too far away. A cell in my block has a radio, and I ask why do they have one and I don't? But when you lash out at the powers that be, you're not going to be rewarded are you. So, what do I do now? Probably just sit here for the rest of the day or maybe I'll go sit over there, it gets more light and it's warmer there when the sun shines, but that's where Percy used to sit so it's a little off putting.

I guess it's midday as that sun is blinding in here now, warm though, nice and warm, I may close my eyes and rest in its glow for a while. Five minutes later Joey fell off his perch. Dead.

CAST

The Elvis - Bobby, 33, Mechanic
The Adolf - Franklin, 44, Drugstore Supervisor
The Jesus - Floyd, 24, Fast Food Technician
The Marilyn - Jodie, 30, Call Girl
The Louis - Henry, 71, Retired Musician
The Groucho - Leonard, 32, Comic Store Clerk
The Host - ???

Bobby's Burger Recipe Ingredients:

1lb (450g) of Minced beef

1 Onion. (Red if preferred)

1 Medium sized egg

6 Sun-dried tomatoes

1/4 Teaspoon of cumin seed

1/4 Teaspoon of cayenne pepper

4 to 6 Slices of cheese (Whatever cheese you prefer)

4 White bread rolls

4 Lettuce leaves

Pinch of salt and pepper

Tomato ketchup or Mustard

Method:

Prep the onion and sun-dried tomatoes by dicing the onion and chopping the sun-dried tomatoes.

Crack the egg and add it to the minced beef and mix together with hands.

Add the diced onion to the mixture and knead.

Add the chopped sun-dried tomatoes and kneed again.

Shape the mixture into patties.

Add a teaspoon of cumin seed mix in and then add the cayenne pepper (just a pinch, not too much)

Place the patties on the grill and cook for a about 4 minutes then flip and cook other side for about another 4 minutes.

Sprinkle some salt and pepper on top.

Top with cheese and then your chosen condiment. And finish with the second bun. Place the lettuce leaf on the base of bun and then add the patty.

I'll Make You Famous

All following stats were correct at the time of writing using Facebook fan/official pages and their amount of

Likes/Follows.

1. Marilyn Monroe 13 million
2. Elvis Presley 12 million
3. Jesus Christ 4.3 million
4. Louis Armstrong 2 million
5. Grouch Marx 4.158 (Marx Bros 127,000)
6. Adolf Hitler 0

HELPFUL DINNER PARTY TIPS

Have a variety of drinks available and always have water available at the table.

Have good quality food available and cater for the needs of your guests.

Some conversation starters...

Who is the most famous person you have met? What is your favourite meal?
What is your favourite film?
What is your favourite smell?
What do you do for a living?
Who is on your celebrity fuck list?
DO NOT murder your guests.

If you could hold a dinner party inviting six famous people who are no longer with us, who would you invite?

Who Would You Invite?

Visit the website www.djbwriter.co.uk

Follow author Daniel J.Barnes on social media
@DJBWriter on Facebook, Instagram & Twitter.

Proud to be part of the Eighty3 Design family. For all your website and graphic design needs.

www.eighty3.co.uk